Dialstone Lane by W. W. Jacobs

William Wymark Jacobs was born on September 8th, 1863 in the Wapping district of London, England. Jacobs grew up near the docks, where his father was a wharf manager.   The docks and river side would be a constant theme of his writing in years to come.

Although surrounded by poverty, he received a formal education in London, first at a private prep school and later at the Birkbeck Literary and Scientific Institute.

His working life began with a less than exciting clerical position at the Post Office Savings Bank. Jacobs put his imagination to good use writing short stories, sketches and articles, many for the Post Office house publication "Blackfriars Magazine."

In 1896 Jacobs published Many Cargoes, a selection of sea-faring yarns, which established him as a popular writer with a knack for authentic dialogue and trick endings.

A year later he published a novelette, The Skipper's Wooing, and in 1898 another collection of short stories; Sea Urchins. These works painted vivid pictures of dockland and seafaring London full of colourful characters.

By 1899, Jacobs was able to quit the post office and write full-time.

He married the noted suffragist Agnes Eleanor Williams (who had been jailed for her protest activities) in 1900. They set up households both in Loughton, Essex and in central London.

The publication in 1902 of At Sunwich Port and Dialstone Lane, in 1904, cemented Jacobs' reputation as one of the leading British authors of the new century.

There followed a string of further successful publications, including Captain's All (1905), Night Watches (1914), The Castaways (1916), and Sea Whispers (1926).

Though Jacobs would create little in the way of new work after 1911, he still wrote and was recognized as a leading humorist, ranked alongside such writers as P. G. Wodehouse.

William Wymark Jacobs died in a North London nursing home in Hornsey Lane, Islington on September 1st, 1943.

Index of Contents

CHAPTER I

Mr. Edward Tredgold sat in the private office of Tredgold and Son, land and estate agents, gazing through the prim wire blinds at the peaceful High Street of Binchester. Tredgold senior, who believed in work for the young, had left early. Tredgold junior, glad at an opportunity of sharing his father's views, had passed most of the work on to a clerk who had arrived in the world exactly three weeks after himself.

"Binchester gets duller and duller," said Mr. Tredgold to himself, wearily. "Two skittish octogenarians, one gloomy baby, one gloomier nursemaid, and three dogs in the last five minutes. If it wasn't for the dogs—Halloa!"

He put down his pen and, rising, looked over the top of the blind at a girl who was glancing from side to side of the road as though in search of an address.

"A visitor," continued Mr. Tredgold, critically. "Girls like that only visit Binchester, and then take the first train back, never to return."

The girl turned at that moment and, encountering the forehead and eyes, gazed at them until they sank slowly behind the protection of the blind.

"She's coming here," said Mr. Tredgold, watching through the wire. "Wants to see our time-table, I expect."

He sat down at the table again, and taking up his pen took some papers from a pigeon-hole and eyed them with severe thoughtfulness.

"A lady to see you, sir," said a clerk, opening the door.

Mr. Tredgold rose and placed a chair.

"I have called for the key of the cottage in Dialstone Lane," said the girl, still standing. "My uncle, Captain Bowers, has not arrived yet, and I am told that you are the landlord."

Mr. Tredgold bowed. "The next train is due at six," he observed, with a glance at the time-table hanging on the wall; "I expect he'll come by that. He was here on Monday seeing the last of the furniture in. Are you Miss Drewitt?"

"Yes," said the girl. "If you'll kindly give me the key, I can go in and wait for him."

Mr. Tredgold took it from a drawer. "If you will allow me, I will go down with you," he said, slowly; "the lock is rather awkward for anybody who doesn't understand it."

The girl murmured something about not troubling him.

"It's no trouble," said Mr. Tredgold, taking up his hat. "It is our duty to do all we can for the comfort of our tenants. That lock—"

He held the door open and followed her into the street, pointing out various objects of interest as they went along.

"I'm afraid you'll find Binchester very quiet," he remarked.

"I like quiet," said his companion.

Mr. Tredgold glanced at her shrewdly, and, pausing only at the jubilee horse-trough to point out beauties which might easily escape any but a trained observation, walked on in silence until they reached their destination.

Except in the matter of window-blinds, Dialstone Lane had not changed for generations, and Mr. Tredgold noted with pleasure the interest of his companion as she gazed at the crumbling roofs, the red-brick doorsteps, and the tiny lattice windows of the cottages. At the last house, a cottage larger than the rest, one side of which bordered the old churchyard, Mr. Tredgold paused and, inserting his key in the lock, turned it with thoughtless ease.

"The lock seems all right; I need not have bothered you," said Miss Drewitt, regarding him gravely.

"Ah, it seems easy," said Mr. Tredgold, shaking his head, "but it wants knack."

The girl closed the door smartly, and, turning the key, opened it again without any difficulty. To satisfy herself—on more points than one—she repeated the performance.

"You've got the knack," said Mr. Tredgold, meeting her gaze with great calmness. "It's extraordinary what a lot of character there is in locks; they let some people open them without any trouble, while others may fumble at them till they're tired."

The girl pushed the door open and stood just inside the room.

"Thank you," she said, and gave him a little bow of dismissal.

A vein of obstinacy in Mr. Tredgold's disposition, which its owner mistook for firmness, asserted itself. It was plain that the girl had estimated his services at their true value and was quite willing to apprise him of the fact. He tried the lock again, and with more bitterness than the occasion seemed to warrant said that somebody had been oiling it.

"I promised Captain Bowers to come in this afternoon and see that a few odd things had been done," he added. "May I come in now?"

The girl withdrew into the room, and, seating herself in a large arm-chair by the fireplace, watched his inspection of door-knobs and window-fastenings with an air of grave amusement, which he found somewhat trying.

"Captain Bowers had the walls panelled and these lockers made to make the room look as much like a ship's cabin as possible," he said, pausing in his labours. "He was quite pleased to find the staircase opening out of the room—he calls it the companion-ladder. And he calls the kitchen the pantry, which led to a lot of confusion with the workmen. Did he tell you of the crow's-nest in the garden?"

"No," said the girl.

"It's a fine piece of work," said Mr. Tredgold.

He opened the door leading into the kitchen and stepped out into the garden. Miss Drewitt, after a moment's hesitation, followed, and after one delighted glance at the trim old garden gazed curiously at a mast with a barrel fixed near the top, which stood at the end.

"There's a fine view from up there," said Mr. Tredgold. "With the captain's glass one can see the sea distinctly. I spent nearly all last Friday afternoon up there, keeping an eye on things. Do you like the garden? Do you think these old creepers ought to be torn down from the house?"

"Certainly not," said Miss Drewitt, with emphasis.

"Just what I said," remarked Mr. Tredgold.

"Captain Bowers wanted to have them pulled down, but I dissuaded him. I advised him to consult you first."

"I don't suppose he really intended to," said the girl.

"He did," said the other, grimly; "said they were untidy. How do you like the way the house is furnished?"

The girl gazed at him for a few moments before replying. "I like it very much," she said, coldly.

"That's right," said Mr. Tredgold, with an air of relief. "You see, I advised the captain what to buy. I went with him to Tollminster and helped him choose. Your room gave me the most anxiety, I think."

"My room?" said the girl, starting.

"It's a dream in the best shades of pink and green," said Mr. Tredgold, modestly. "Pink on the walls, and carpets and hangings green; three or four bits of old furniture—the captain objected, but I stood firm; and for pictures I had two or three little things out of an art journal framed."

"Is furnishing part of your business?" inquired the girl, eyeing him in bewilderment.

"Business?" said the other. "Oh, no. I did it for amusement. I chose and the captain paid. It was a delightful experience. The sordid question of price was waived; for once expense was nothing to me. I wish you'd just step up to your room and see how you like it. It's the one over the kitchen."

Miss Drewitt hesitated, and then curiosity, combined with a cheerful idea of probably being able to disapprove of the lauded decorations, took her indoors and upstairs. In a few minutes she came down again.

"I suppose it's all right," she said, ungraciously, "but I don't understand why you should have selected it."

"I had to," said Mr. Tredgold, confidentially. "I happened to go to Tollminster the same day as the captain and went into a shop with him. If you could only see the things he wanted to buy, you would understand."

The girl was silent.

"The paper the captain selected for your room," continued Mr. Tredgold, severely, "was decorated with branches of an unknown flowering shrub, on the top twig of which a humming-bird sat eating a dragonfly. A rough calculation showed me that every time you opened your eyes in the morning you would see fifty-seven humming-birds-all made in the same pattern-eating fifty-seven ditto dragon-flies. The captain said it was cheerful."

"I have no doubt that my uncle's selection would have satisfied me," said Miss Drewitt, coldly.

"The curtains he fancied were red, with small yellow tigers crouching all over them," pursued Mr. Tredgold. "The captain seemed fond of animals."

"I think that you were rather—venturesome," said the girl. "Suppose that I had not liked the things you selected?"

Mr. Tredgold deliberated. "I felt sure that you would like them," he said, at last. "It was a hard struggle not to keep some of the things for myself. I've had my eye on those two Chippendale chairs for years. They belonged to an old woman in Mint Street, but she always refused to part with them. I shouldn't have got them, only one of them let her down the other day."

"Let her down?" repeated Miss Drewitt, sharply. "Do you mean one of the chairs in my bedroom?"

Mr. Tredgold nodded. "Gave her rather a nasty fall," he said. "I struck while the iron was hot, and went and made her an offer while she was still laid up from the effects of it. It's the one standing against the wall; the other's all right, with proper care."

Miss Drewitt, after a somewhat long interval, thanked him.

"You must have been very useful to my uncle," she said, slowly. "I feel sure that he would never have bought chairs like those of his own accord."

"He has been at sea all his life," said Mr. Tredgold, in extenuation. You haven't seen him for a long time, have you?"

"Ten years," was the reply.

"He is delightful company," said Mr. Tredgold. "His life has been one long series of adventures in every quarter of the globe. His stock of yarns is like the widow's cruse. And here he comes," he added, as a dilapidated fly drew up at the house and an elderly man, with a red, weatherbeaten face, partly hidden in a cloud of grey beard, stepped out and stood in the doorway, regarding the girl with something almost akin to embarrassment.

"It's not—not Prudence?" he said at length, holding out his hand and staring at her.

"Yes, uncle," said the girl.

They shook hands, and Captain Bowers, reaching up for a cage containing a parrot, which had been noisily entreating the cabman for a kiss all the way from the station, handed that flustered person his fare and entered the house again.

"Glad to see you, my lad," he said, shaking hands with Mr. Tredgold and glancing covertly at his niece. "I hope you haven't been waiting long," he added, turning to the latter.

"No," said Miss Drewitt, regarding him with a puzzled air.

"I missed the train," said the captain. "We must try and manage better next time. I0-I hope you'll be comfortable."

"Thank you," said the girl.

"You—you are very like your poor mother," said the captain.

"I hope so," said Prudence.

She stole up to the captain and, after a moment's hesitation, kissed his cheek. The next moment she was caught up and crushed in the arms of a powerful and affectionate bear.

"Blest if I hardly knew how to take you at first," said the captain, his red face shining with gratification.

"Little girls are one thing, but when they grow up into"—he held her away and looked at her proudly—"into handsome and dignified-looking young women, a man doesn't quite know where he is." He took her in his arms again and, kissing her forehead, winked delightedly in the direction of Mr. Tredgold, who was affecting to look out of the window.

"My man'll be in soon," he said, releasing the girl, "and then we'll see about some tea. He met me at the station and I sent him straight off for things to eat."

"Your man?" said Miss Drewitt.

"Yes; I thought a man would be easier to manage than a girl," said the captain, knowingly. "You can be freer with 'em in the matter of language, and then there's no followers or anything of that kind. I got him to sign articles ship-shape and proper. Mr. Tredgold recommended him."

"No, no," said that gentleman, hastily.

"I asked you before he signed on with me," said the captain, pointing a stumpy forefinger at him. "I made a point of it, and you told me that you had never heard anything against him."

"I don't call that a recommendation," said Mr. Tredgold.

"It's good enough in these days," retorted the captain, gloomily. "A man that has got a character like that is hard to find."

"He might be artful and keep his faults to himself," suggested Tredgold.

"So long as he does that, it's all right," said Captain Bowers. "I can't find fault if there's no faults to find fault with. The best steward I ever had, I found out afterwards, had escaped from gaol. He never wanted to go ashore, and when the ship was in port almost lived in his pantry."

"I never heard of Tasker having been in gaol," said Mr. Tredgold. "Anyhow, I'm certain that he never broke out of one; he's far too stupid."

As he paid this tribute the young man referred to entered laden with parcels, and, gazing awkwardly at the company, passed through the room on tiptoe and began to busy himself in the pantry. Mr. Tredgold, refusing the captain's invitation to stay for a cup of tea, took his departure.

"Very nice youngster that," said the captain, looking after him. "A little bit light-hearted in his ways, perhaps, but none the worse for that."

He sat down and looked round at his possessions. "The first real home I've had for nearly fifty years," he said, with great content. "I hope you'll be as happy here as I intend to be. It sha'n't be my fault if you're not."

Mr. Tredgold walked home deep in thought, and by the time he had arrived there had come to the conclusion that if Miss Drewitt favoured her mother, that lady must have been singularly unlike Captain Bowers in features.

CHAPTER II

In less than a week Captain Bowers had settled down comfortably in his new command. A set of rules and regulations by which Mr. Joseph Tasker was to order his life was framed and hung in the pantry. He studied it with care, and, anxious that there should be no possible chance of a misunderstanding, questioned the spelling in three instances. The captain's explanation that he had spelt those words in the American style was an untruthful reflection upon a great and friendly nation.

Dialstone Lane was at first disposed to look askance at Mr. Tasker. Old-fashioned matrons clustered round to watch him cleaning the doorstep, and, surprised at its whiteness, withdrew discomfited. Rumour had it that he liked work, and scandal said that he had wept because he was not allowed to do the washing.

The captain attributed this satisfactory condition of affairs to the rules and regulations, though a slight indiscretion on the part of Mr. Tasker, necessitating the unframing of the document to add to the latter, caused him a little annoyance.

The first intimation he had of it was a loud knocking at the front door as he sat dozing one afternoon in his easy-chair. In response to his startled cry of "Come in!" the door opened and a small man, in a state of considerable agitation, burst into the room and confronted him.

"My name is Chalk," he said, breathlessly.

"A friend of Mr. Tredgold's?" said the captain. "I've heard of you, sir."

The visitor paid no heed.

"My wife wishes to know whether she has got to dress in the dark every afternoon for the rest of her life," he said, in fierce but trembling tones.

"Got to dress in the dark?" repeated the astonished captain.

"With the blind down," explained the other.

Captain Bowers looked him up and down. He saw a man of about fifty nervously fingering the little bits of fluffy red whisker which grew at the sides of his face, and trying to still the agitation of his tremulous mouth.

"How would you like it yourself?" demanded the visitor, whose manner was gradually becoming milder and milder. "How would you like a telescope a yard long pointing—"

He broke off abruptly as the captain, with a smothered oath, dashed out of his chair into the garden and stood shaking his fist at the crow's-nest at the bottom.

"Joseph!" he bawled.

"Yes, sir," said Mr. Tasker, removing the telescope described by Mr. Chalk from his eye, and leaning over.

"What are you doing with that spy-glass?" demanded his master, beckoning to the visitor, who had drawn near. "How dare you stare in at people's windows?"

"I wasn't, sir," replied Mr. Tasker, in an injured voice. "I wouldn't think o' such a thing—I couldn't, not if I tried."

"You'd got it pointed straight at my bedroom window," cried Mr. Chalk, as he accompanied the captain down the garden. "And it ain't the first time."

"I wasn't, sir," said the steward, addressing his master. "I was watching the martins under the eaves."

"You'd got it pointed at my window," persisted the visitor.

"That's where the nests are," said Mr. Tasker, "but I wasn't looking in at the window. Besides, I noticed you always pulled the blind down when you saw me looking, so I thought it didn't matter."

"We can't do anything without being followed about by that telescope," said Mr. Chalk, turning to the captain. "My wife had our house built where it is on purpose, so that we shouldn't be overlooked. We didn't bargain for a thing like that sprouting up in a back-garden."

"I'm very sorry," said the captain. "I wish you'd told me of it before. If I catch you up there again," he cried, shaking his fist at Mr. Tasker, "you'll remember it. Come down!"

Mr. Tasker, placing the glass under his arm, came slowly and reluctantly down the ratlines.

"I wasn't looking in at the window, Mr. Chalk," he said, earnestly. "I was watching the birds. O' course, I couldn't help seeing in a bit, but I always shifted the spy-glass at once if there was anything that I thought I oughtn't—"

"That'll do," broke in the captain, hastily. "Go in and get the tea ready. If I so much as see you looking at that glass again we part, my lad, mind that."

"I don't suppose he meant any harm," said the mollified Mr. Chalk, after the crestfallen Joseph had gone into the house. "I hope I haven't been and said too much, but my wife insisted on me coming round and speaking about it."

"You did quite right," said the captain, "and I thank you for coming. I told him he might go up there occasionally, but I particularly warned him against giving any annoyance to the neighbours."

"I suppose," said Mr. Chalk, gazing at the erection with interest— "I suppose there's a good view from up there? It's like having a ship in the garden, and it seems to remind you of the North Pole, and whales, and Northern Lights."

Five minutes later Mr. Tasker, peering through the pantry window, was surprised to see Mr. Chalk ascending with infinite caution to the crow's-nest. His high hat was jammed firmly over his brows and the telescope was gripped tightly under his right arm. The journey was evidently regarded as one of extreme peril by the climber; but he held on gallantly and, arrived at the top, turned a tremulous telescope on to the horizon.

Mr. Tasker took a deep breath and resumed his labours. He set the table, and when the water boiled made the tea, and went down the garden to announce the fact. Mr. Chalk was still up aloft, and even at that height the pallor of his face was clearly discernible. It was evident to the couple below that the terrors of the descent were too much for him, but that he was too proud to say so.

"Nice view up there," called the captain.

"B—b—beautiful," cried Mr. Chalk, with an attempt at enthusiasm.

The captain paced up and down impatiently; his tea was getting cold, but the forlorn figure aloft made no sign. The captain waited a little longer, and then, laying hold of the shrouds, slowly mounted until his head was above the platform.

"Shall I take the glass for you?" he inquired.

Mr. Chalk, clutching the edge of the cask, leaned over and handed it down.

"My—my foot's gone to sleep," he stammered.

"Ho! Well, you must be careful how you get down," said the captain, climbing on to the platform. "Now, gently."

He put the telescope back into the cask, and, beckoning Mr. Tasker to ascend, took Mr. Chalk in a firm grasp and lowered him until he was able to reach Mr. Tasker's face with his foot. After that the descent was easy, and Mr. Chalk, reaching ground once more, spent two or three minutes in slapping and rubing, and other remedies prescribed for sleepy feet.

"There's few gentlemen that would have come down at all with their foot asleep," remarked Mr. Tasker, pocketing a shilling, when the captain's back was turned.

Mr. Chalk, still pale and shaking somewhat, smiled feebly and followed the captain into the house. The latter offered a cup of tea, which the visitor, after a faint protest, accepted, and taking a seat at the table gazed in undisguised admiration at the nautical appearance of the room.

"I could fancy myself aboard ship," he declared.

"Are you fond of the sea?" inquired the captain.

"I love it," said Mr. Chalk, fervently. "It was always my idea from a boy to go to sea, but somehow I didn't. I went into my father's business instead, but I never liked it. Some people are fond of a stay-at-home life, but I always had a hankering after adventures."

The captain shook his head. "Ha!" he said, impressively.

"You've had a few in your time," said Mr. Chalk, looking at him, grudgingly; "Edward Tredgold was telling me so."

"Man and boy, I was at sea forty-nine years," remarked the captain. "Naturally things happened in that time; it would have been odd if they hadn't. It's all in a lifetime."

"Some lifetimes," said Mr. Chalk, gloomily. "I'm fifty-one next year, and the only thing I ever had happen to me was seeing a man stop a runaway horse and cart."

He shook his head solemnly over his monotonous career, and, gazing at a war-club from Samoa which hung over the fireplace, put a few leading questions to the captain concerning the manner in which it came into his possession. When Prudence came in half an hour later he was still sitting there, listening with rapt attention to his host's tales of distant seas.

It was the first of many visits. Sometimes he brought Mr. Tredgold and sometimes Mr. Tredgold brought him. The terrors of the crow's-nest vanished before his persevering attacks, and perched there with the captain's glass he swept the landscape with the air of an explorer surveying a strange and hostile country.

It was a fitting prelude to the captain's tales afterwards, and Mr. Chalk, with the stem of his long pipe withdrawn from his open mouth, would sit enthralled as his host narrated picturesque incidents of hairbreadth escapes, or, drawing his chair to the table, made rough maps for his listener's clearer understanding. Sometimes the captain took him to palm-studded islands in the Southern Seas; sometimes to the ancient worlds of China and Japan. He became an expert in nautical terms. He walked in knots, and even ordered a new carpet in fathoms—after the shop-keeper had demonstrated, by means of his little boy's arithmetic book, the difference between that measurement and a furlong.

"I'll have a voyage before I'm much older," he remarked one afternoon, as he sat in the captain's sitting-room. "Since I retired from business time hangs very heavy sometimes. I've got a fancy for a small yacht, but I suppose I couldn't go a long voyage in a small one?"

"Smaller the better," said Edward Tredgold, who was sitting by the window watching Miss Drewitt sewing.

Mr. Chalk took his pipe from his mouth and eyed him inquiringly.

"Less to lose," explained Mr. Tredgold, with a scarcely perceptible glance at the captain. "Look at the dangers you'd be dragging your craft into, Chalk; there would be no satisfying you with a quiet cruise in the Mediterranean."

"I shouldn't run into unnecessary danger," said Mr. Chalk, seriously. "I'm a married man, and there's my wife to think of. What would become of her if anything happened to me?"

"Why, you've got plenty of money to leave, haven't you?" inquired Mr. Tredgold.

"I was thinking of her losing me," replied Mr. Chalk, with a touch of acerbity.

"Oh, I didn't think of that," said the other. "Yes, to be sure."

"Captain Bowers was telling me the other day of a woman who wore widow's weeds for thirty-five years," said Mr. Chalk, impressively. "And all the time her husband was married again and got a big family in Australia. There's nothing in the world so faithful as a woman's heart."

"Well, if you're lost on a cruise, I shall know where to look for you," said Mr. Tredgold. "But I don't think the captain ought to put such ideas into your head."

Mr. Chalk looked bewildered. Then he scratched his left whisker with the stem of his churchwarden pipe and looked severely over at Mr. Tredgold.

"I don't think you ought to talk that way before ladies," he said, primly. "Of course, I know you're only in joke, but there's some people can't see jokes as quick as others and they might get a wrong idea of you."

"What part did you think of going to for your cruise?" interposed Captain Bowers.

"There's nothing settled yet," said Mr. Chalk; "it's just an idea, that's all. I was talking to your father the other day," he added, turning to Mr. Tredgold; "just sounding him, so to speak."

"You take him," said that dutiful son, briskly. "It would do him a world of good; me, too."

"He said he couldn't afford either the time or the money," said Mr. Chalk. "The thing to do would be to combine business with pleasure—to take a yacht and find a sunken galleon loaded with gold pieces. I've heard of such things being done."

"I've heard of it," said the captain, nodding.

"Bottom of the ocean must be paved with them in places," said Mr. Tredgold, rising, and following Miss Drewitt, who had gone into the garden to plant seeds.

Mr. Chalk refilled his pipe and, accepting a match from the captain, smoked slowly. His gaze was fixed on the window, but instead of Dialstone Lane he saw tumbling blue seas and islets far away.

"That's something you've never come across, I suppose, Captain Bowers?" he remarked at last.

"No," said the other.

Mr. Chalk, with a vain attempt to conceal his disappointment, smoked on for some time in silence. The blue seas disappeared, and he saw instead the brass knocker of the house opposite.

"Nor any other kind of craft with treasure aboard, I suppose?" he suggested, at last.

The captain put his hands on his knees and stared at the floor. "No," he said, slowly, "I can't call to mind any craft; but it's odd that you should have got on this subject with me."

Mr. Chalk laid his pipe carefully on the table.

"Why?" he inquired.

"Well," said the captain, with a short laugh, "it is odd, that's all."

Mr. Chalk fidgeted with the stem of his pipe. "You know of sunken treasure somewhere?" he said, eagerly.

The captain smiled and shook his head; the other watched him narrowly.

"You know of some treasure?" he said, with conviction.

"Not what you could call sunken," said the captain, driven to bay.

Mr. Chalk's pale-blue eyes opened to their fullest extent. "Ingots?" he queried.

The other shook his head. "It's a secret," he remarked; "we won't talk about it."

"Yes, of course, naturally, I don't expect you to tell me where it is," said Mr. Chalk, "but I thought it might be interesting to hear about, that's all."

"It's buried," said the captain, after a long pause. "I don't know that there's any harm in telling you that; buried in a small island in the South Pacific."

"Have you seen it?" inquired Mr. Chalk.

"I buried it," rejoined the other.

Mr. Chalk sank back in his chair and regarded him with awestruck attention; Captain Bowers, slowly ramming home a charge of tobacco with his thumb, smiled quietly.

"Buried it," he repeated, musingly, "with the blade of an oar for a spade. It was a long job, but it's six foot down and the dead man it belonged to atop of it."

The pipe fell from the listener's fingers and smashed unheeded on the floor.

"You ought to make a book of it," he said at last.

The captain shook his head. "I haven't got the gift of story-telling," he said, simply. "Besides, you can understand I don't want it noised about. People might bother me."

He leaned back in his chair and bunched his beard in his hand; the other, watching him closely, saw that his thoughts were busy with some scene in his stirring past.

"Not a friend of yours, I hope?" said Mr. Chalk, at last.

"Who?" inquired the captain, starting from his reverie.

"The dead man atop of the treasure," replied the other.

"No," said the captain, briefly.

"Is it worth much?" asked Mr. Chalk.

"Roughly speaking, about half a million," responded the captain, calmly.

Mr. Chalk rose and walked up and down the room. His eyes were bright and his face pinker than usual.

"Why don't you get it?" he demanded, at last, pausing in front of his host.

"Why, it ain't mine," said the captain, staring. "D'ye think I'm a thief?"

Mr. Chalk stared in his turn. "But who does it belong to, then?" he inquired.

"I don't know," replied the captain. "All I know is, it isn't mine, and that's enough for me. Whether it was rightly come by I don't know. There it is, and there it'll stay till the crack of doom."

"Don't you know any of his relations or friends?" persisted the other.

"I know nothing of him except his name," said the captain, "and I doubt if even that was his right one. Don Silvio he called himself—a Spaniard. It's over ten years ago since it happened. My ship had been bought by a firm in Sydney, and while I was waiting out there I went for a little run on a schooner among the islands. This Don Silvio was aboard of her as a passenger. She went to pieces in a gale, and we were the only two saved. The others were washed overboard, but we got ashore in the boat, and I thought from the trouble he was taking over his bag that the danger had turned his brain."

"Ah!" said the keenly interested Mr. Chalk.

"He was a sick man aboard ship," continued the captain, "and I soon saw that he hadn't saved his life for long. He saw it, too, and before he died he made me promise that the bag should be buried with him and never disturbed. After I'd promised, he opened the bag and showed me what was in it. It was full of precious stones—diamonds, rubies, and the like; some of them as large as birds' eggs. I can see him now, propped up against the boat and playing with them in the sunlight. They blazed like stars. Half a million he put them at, or more."

"What good could they be to him when he was dead?" inquired the listener.

Captain Bowers shook his head. "That was his business, not mine," he replied. "It was nothing to do with me. When he died I dug a grave for him, as I told you, with a bit of a broken oar, and laid him and the bag together. A month afterwards I was taken off by a passing schooner and landed safe at Sydney."

Mr. Chalk stopped, and mechanically picking up the pieces of his pipe placed them on the table.

"Suppose that you had heard afterwards that the things had been stolen?" he remarked.

"If I had, then I should have given information, I think," said the other. "It all depends."

"Ah! but how could you have found them again?" inquired Mr. Chalk, with the air of one propounding a poser.

"With my map," said the captain, slowly. "Before I left I made a map of the island and got its position from the schooner that picked me up; but I never heard a word from that day to this."

"Could you find them now?" said Mr. Chalk.

"Why not?" said the captain, with a short laugh. "The island hasn't run away."

He rose as he spoke and, tossing the fragments of his visitor's pipe into the fireplace, invited him to take a turn in the garden. Mr. Chalk, after a feeble attempt to discuss the matter further, reluctantly obeyed.

CHAPTER III

Mr. Chalk, with his mind full of the story he had just heard, walked homewards like a man in a dream. The air was fragrant with spring and the scent of lilac revived memories almost forgotten. It took him back forty years, and showed him a small boy treading the same road, passing the same houses. Nothing had changed so much as the small boy himself; nothing had been so unlike the life he had pictured as the life he had led. Even the blamelessness of the latter yielded no comfort; it savoured of a lack of spirit.

His mind was still busy with the past when he reached home. Mrs. Chalk, a woman of imposing appearance, who was sitting by the window at needlework, looked up sharply at his entrance. Before she spoke he had a dim idea that she was excited about something.

"I've got her," she said, triumphantly.

"Oh!" said Mr. Chalk.

"She didn't want to come at first," said Mrs. Chalk; "she'd half promised to go to Mrs. Morris. Mrs. Morris had heard of her through Harris, the grocer, and he only knew she was out of a place by accident. He—"

Her words fell on deaf ears. Mr. Chalk, gazing through the window, heard without comprehending a long account of the capture of a new housemaid, which, slightly altered as to name and place, would have passed muster as an exciting contest between a skilful angler and a particularly sulky salmon. Mrs. Chalk, noticing his inattention at last, pulled up sharply.

"You're not listening!" she cried.

"Yes, I am; go on, my dear," said Mr. Chalk.

"What did I say she left her last place for, then?" demanded the lady.

Mr. Chalk started. He had been conscious of his wife's voice, and that was all. "You said you were not surprised at her leaving," he replied, slowly; "the only wonder to you was that a decent girl should have stayed there so long."

Mrs. Chalk started and bit her lip. "Yes," she said, slowly. "Ye-es. Go on; anything else?"

"You said the house wanted cleaning from top to bottom," said the painstaking Mr. Chalk.

"Go on," said his wife, in a smothered voice. "What else did I say?"

"Said you pitied the husband," continued Mr. Chalk, thoughtfully.

Mrs. Chalk rose suddenly and stood over him. Mr. Chalk tried desperately to collect his faculties.

"How dare you?" she gasped. "I've never said such things in my life. Never. And I said that she left because Mr. Wilson, her master, was dead and the family had gone to London. I've never been near the house; so how could I say such things?"

Mr. Chalk remained silent.

"What made you think of such things?" persisted Mrs. Chalk.

Mr. Chalk shook his head; no satisfactory reply was possible. "My thoughts were far away," he said, at last.

His wife bridled and said, "Oh, indeed!" Mr. Chalk's mother, dead some ten years before, had taken a strange pride—possibly as a protest against her only son's appearance—in hinting darkly at a stormy and chequered past. Pressed for details she became more mysterious still, and, saying that "she knew what she knew," declined to be deprived of the knowledge under any consideration. She also informed her daughter-in-law that "what the eye don't see the heart don't grieve," and that it was better to "let bygones be bygones," usually winding up with the advice to the younger woman to keep her eye on Mr. Chalk without letting him see it.

"Peckham Rye is a long way off, certainly," added the indignant Mrs. Chalk, after a pause. "It's a pity you haven't got something better to think of, at your time of life, too."

Mr. Chalk flushed. Peckham Rye was one of the nuisances bequeathed by his mother.

"I was thinking of the sea," he said, loftily.

Mrs. Chalk pounced. "Oh, Yarmouth," she said, with withering scorn.

Mr. Chalk flushed deeper than before. "I wasn't thinking of such things," he declared.

"What things?" said his wife, swiftly.

"The—the things you're alluding to," said the harassed Mr. Chalk.

"Ah!" said his wife, with a toss of her head. "Why you should get red in the face and confused when I say Peckham Rye and Yarmouth are a long way off is best known to yourself. It's very funny that the moment either of these places is mentioned you get uncomfortable. People might read a geography-book out loud in my presence and it wouldn't affect me."

She swept out of the room, and Mr. Chalk's thoughts, excited by the magic word geography, went back to the island again. The half-forgotten dreams of his youth appeared to be materializing. Sleepy Binchester ended for him at Dialstone Lane, and once inside the captain's room the enchanted world beyond the seas was spread before his eager gaze. The captain, amused at first at his enthusiasm, began to get weary of the subject of the island, and so far the visitor had begged in vain for a glimpse of the map.

His enthusiasm became contagious. Prudence, entering one evening in the middle of a conversation, heard sufficient to induce her to ask for more, and the captain, not without some reluctance and several promptings from Mr. Chalk when he showed signs of omitting vital points, related the story. Edward Tredgold heard it, and, judging by the frequency of his visits, was almost as interested as Mr. Chalk.

"I can't see that there could be any harm in just looking at the map," said Mr. Chalk, one evening. "You could keep your thumb on any part you wanted to."

"Then we should know where to dig," urged Mr. Tredgold. "Properly managed there ought to be a fortune in your innocence, Chalk."

Mr. Chalk eyed him fixedly. "Seeing that the latitude and longitude and all the directions are written on the back," he observed, with cold dignity, "I don't see the force of your remarks."

"Well, in that case, why not show it to Mr. Chalk, uncle?" said Prudence, charitably.

Captain Bowers began to show signs of annoyance. "Well, my dear," he began, slowly.

"Then Miss Drewitt could see it too," said Mr. Tredgold, blandly.

Miss Drewitt reddened with indignation. "I could see it any time I wished," she said, sharply.

"Well, wish now," entreated Mr. Tredgold. "As a matter of fact, I'm dying with curiosity myself. Bring it out and make it crackle, captain; it's a bank-note for half a million."

The captain shook his head and a slight frown marred his usually amiable features. He got up and, turning his back on them, filled his pipe from a jar on the mantelpiece.

"You never will see it, Chalk," said Edward Tredgold, in tones of much conviction. "I'll bet you two to one in golden sovereigns that you'll sink into your honoured family vault with your justifiable curiosity still unsatisfied. And I shouldn't wonder if your perturbed spirit walks the captain's bedroom afterwards."

Miss Drewitt looked up and eyed the speaker with scornful comprehension. "Take the bet, Mr. Chalk," she said, slowly.

Mr. Chalk turned in hopeful amaze; then he leaned over and shook hands solemnly with Mr. Tredgold. "I'll take the bet," he said.

"Uncle will show it to you to please me," announced Prudence, in a clear voice. "Won't you, uncle?"

The captain turned and took the matches from the table. "Certainly, my dear, if I can find it," he said, in a hesitating fashion. "But I'm afraid I've mislaid it. I haven't seen it since I unpacked."

"Mislaid it!" ejaculated the startled Mr. Chalk. "Good heavens! Suppose somebody should find it? What about your word to Don Silvio then?"

"I've got it somewhere," said the captain, brusquely; "I'll have a hunt for it. All the same, I don't know that it's quite fair to interfere in a bet."

Miss Drewitt waved the objection away, remarking that people who made bets must risk losing their money.

"I'll begin to save up," said Mr. Tredgold, with a lightness which was not lost upon Miss Drewitt. "The captain has got to find it before you can see it, Chalk."

Mr. Chalk, with a satisfied smile, said that when the captain promised a thing it was as good as done.

For the next few days he waited patiently, and, ransacking an old lumber-room, divided his time pretty equally between a volume of "Captain Cook's Voyages" that he found there and "Famous Shipwrecks." By this means and the exercise of great self-control he ceased from troubling Dialstone Lane for a week. Even then it was Edward Tredgold who took him there. The latter was in high spirits, and in explanation informed the company, with a cheerful smile, that he had saved five and ninepence, and was forming habits which bade fair to make him a rich man in time.

"Don't you be in too much of a hurry to find that map, captain," he said.

"It's found," said Miss Drewitt, with a little note of triumph in her voice.

"Found it this morning," said Captain Bowers. He crossed over to an oak bureau which stood in the corner by the fireplace, and taking a paper from a pigeon-hole slowly unfolded it and spread it on the table before the delighted Mr. Chalk. Miss Drewitt and Edward Tredgold advanced to the table and eyed it curiously.

The map, which was drawn in lead-pencil, was on a piece of ruled paper, yellow with age and cracked in the folds. The island was in shape a rough oval, the coast-line being broken by small bays and headlands. Mr. Chalk eyed it with all the fervour usually bestowed on a holy relic, and, breathlessly reading off such terms as "Cape Silvio," "Bowers Bay," and "Mount Lonesome," gazed with breathless interest at the discoverer.

"And is that the grave?" he inquired, in a trembling voice, pointing to a mark in the north-east corner.

The captain removed it with his finger-nail. "No," he said, briefly. "For full details see the other side."

For one moment Mr. Chalk hoped; then his face fell as Captain Bowers, displaying for a fraction of a second the writing on the other side, took up the map and, replacing it in the bureau, turned the key in the lock and with a low laugh resumed his seat. Miss Drewitt, glancing over at Edward Tredgold, saw that he looked very thoughtful.

"You've lost your bet," she said, pointedly.

"I know," was the reply.

His gaiety had vanished and he looked so dejected that Miss Drewitt was reminded of the ruined gambler in a celebrated picture. She tried to quiet her conscience by hoping that it would be a lesson to him. As she watched, Mr. Tredgold dived into his left trouser-pocket and counted out some coins, mostly brown. To these he added a few small pieces of silver gleaned from his waistcoat, and then after a few seconds' moody thought found a few more in the other trouser-pocket.

"Eleven and tenpence," he said, mechanically.

"Any time," said Mr. Chalk, regarding him with awkward surprise. "Any time."

"Give him an I O U," said Captain Bowers, fidgeting.

"Yes, any time," repeated Mr. Chalk; "I'm in no hurry."

"No; I'd sooner pay now and get it over," said the other, still fumbling in his pockets. "As Miss Drewitt says, people who make bets must be prepared to lose; I thought I had more than this."

There was an embarrassing silence, during which Miss Drewitt, who had turned very red, felt strangely uncomfortable. She felt more uncomfortable still when Mr. Tredgold, discovering a bank-note and a little collection of gold coins in another pocket, artlessly expressed his joy at the discovery. The simple-minded captain and Mr. Chalk both experienced a sense of relief; Miss Drewitt sat and simmered in helpless indignation.

"You're careless in money matters, my lad," said the captain, reprovingly.

"I couldn't understand him making all that fuss over a couple o' pounds," said Mr. Chalk, looking round. "He's very free, as a rule; too free."

Mr. Tredgold, sitting grave and silent, made no reply to these charges, and the girl was the only one to notice a faint twitching at the corners of his mouth. She saw it distinctly, despite the fact that her clear, grey eyes were fixed dreamily on a spot some distance above his head.

She sat in her room upstairs after the visitors had gone, thinking it over. The light was fading fast, and as she sat at the open window the remembrance of Mr. Tredgold's conduct helped to mar one of the most perfect evenings she had ever known.

Downstairs the captain was also thinking. Dialstone Lane was in shadow, and already one or two lamps were lit behind drawn blinds. A little chatter of voices at the end of the lane floated in at the open window, mellowed by distance. His pipe was out, and he rose to search in the gloom for a match, when another murmur of voices reached his ears from the kitchen. He stood still and listened intently. To put matters beyond all doubt, the shrill laugh of a girl was plainly audible. The captain's face hardened, and, crossing to the fireplace, he rang the bell.

"Yessir," said Joseph, as he appeared and closed the door carefully behind him.

"What are you talking to yourself in that absurd manner for?" inquired the captain with great dignity.

"Me, sir?" said Mr. Tasker, feebly.

"Yes, you," repeated the captain, noticing with surprise that the door was slowly opening.

Mr. Tasker gazed at him in a troubled fashion, but made no reply.

"I won't have it," said the captain, sternly, with a side glance at the door. "If you want to talk to yourself go outside and do it. I never heard such a laugh. What did you do it for? It was like an old woman with a bad cold."

He smiled grimly in the darkness, and then started slightly as a cough, a hostile, challenging cough, sounded from the kitchen. Before he could speak the cough ceased and a thin voice broke carelessly into song.

"WHAT!" roared the captain, in well-feigned astonishment. "Do you mean to tell me you've got somebody in my pantry? Go and get me those rules and regulations."

Mr. Tasker backed out, and the captain smiled again as he heard a whispered discussion. Then a voice clear and distinct took command. "I'll take 'em in myself, I tell you," it said. "I'll rules and regulations him."

The smile faded from the captain's face, and he gazed in perplexity at the door as a strange young woman bounced into the room.

"Here's your rules and regulations," said the intruder, in a somewhat shrewish voice. "You'd better light the lamp if you want to see 'em; though the spelling ain't so noticeable in the dark."

The impressiveness of the captain's gaze was wasted in the darkness. For a moment he hesitated, and then, with the dignity of a man whose spelling has nothing to conceal, struck a match and lit the lamp. The lamp lighted, he lowered the blind, and then seating himself by the window turned with a majestic air to a thin slip of a girl with tow-coloured hair, who stood by the door.

"Who are you?" he demanded, gruffly.

"My name's Vickers," said the young lady. "Selina Vickers. I heard all what you've been saying to my Joseph, but, thank goodness, I can take my own part. I don't want nobody to fight my battles for me. If you've got anything to say about my voice you can say it to my face."

Captain Bowers sat back and regarded her with impressive dignity. Miss Vickers met his gaze calmly and, with a pair of unwinking green eyes, stared him down.

"What were you doing in my pantry?" demanded the captain, at last.

"I was in your kitchen," replied Miss Vickers, with scornful emphasis on the last word, "to see my young man."

"Well, I can't have you there," said the captain, with a mildness that surprised himself. "One of my rules—"

Miss Vickers interposed. "I've read 'em all over and over again," she said, impatiently.

"If it occurs again," said the other, "I shall have to speak to Joseph very seriously about it."

"Talk to me," said Miss Vickers, sharply; "that's what I come in for. I can talk to you better than what Joseph can, I know. What harm do you think I was doing your old kitchen? Don't you try and interfere between me and my Joseph, because I won't have it. You're not married yourself, and you don't want other people to be. How do you suppose the world would get on if everybody was like you?"

Captain Bowers regarded her in open-eyed perplexity. The door leading to the garden had just closed behind the valiant Joseph, and he stared with growing uneasiness at the slight figure of Miss Vickers as it stood poised for further oratorical efforts. Before he could speak she gave her lips a rapid lick and started again.

"You're one of those people that don't like to see others happy, that's what you are," she said, rapidly. "I wasn't hurting your kitchen, and as to talking and laughing there—what do you think my tongue was given to me for? Show? P'r'aps if you'd been doing a day's hard work you'd—"

"Look here, my girl—" began the captain, desperately.

"Don't you my girl me, please," interrupted Miss Vickers. "I'm not your girl, thank goodness. If I was you'd be a bit different, I can tell you. If you had any girls you'd know better than to try and come between them and their young men. Besides, they wouldn't let you. When a girl's got a young man—"

The captain rose and went through the form of ringing the bell. Miss Vickers watched him calmly.

"I thought I'd just have it out with you for once and for all," she continued. "I told Joseph that I'd no doubt your bark was worse than your bite. And what he can see to be afraid of in you I can't think. Nervous disposition, I s'pose. Good evening."

She gave her head a little toss and, returning to the pantry, closed the door after her. Captain Bowers, still somewhat dazed, returned to his chair and, gazing at the "Rules," which still lay on the table, grinned feebly in his beard.

CHAPTER IV

To keep such a romance to himself was beyond the powers of Mr. Chalk. The captain had made no conditions as to secrecy, and he therefore considered himself free to indulge in hints to his two greatest friends, which caused those gentlemen to entertain some doubts as to his sanity. Mr. Robert Stobell, whose work as a contractor had left a permanent and unmistakable mark upon Binchester, became imbued with a hazy idea that Mr. Chalk had invented a new process of making large diamonds. Mr. Jasper Tredgold, on the other hand, arrived at the conclusion that a highly respectable burglar was offering for some reason to share his loot with him. A conversation between Messrs. Stobell and Tredgold in the High Street only made matters more complicated.

"Chalk always was fond of making mysteries of things," complained Mr. Tredgold.

Mr. Stobell, whose habit was taciturn and ruminative, fixed his dull brown eyes on the ground and thought it over. "I believe it's all my eye and Betty Martin," he said, at length, quoting a saying which had been used in his family as an expression of disbelief since the time of his great-grandmother.

"He comes in to see me when I'm hard at work and drops hints," pursued his friend. "When I stop to pick 'em up, out he goes. Yesterday he came in and asked me what I thought of a man who wouldn't break his word for half a million. Half a million, mind you! I just asked him who it was, and out he went again. He pops in and out of my office like a figure on a cuckoo-clock."

Mr. Stobell relapsed into thought again, but no gleam of expression disturbed the lines of his heavy face; Mr. Tredgold, whose sharp, alert features bred more confidence in his own clients than those of other people, waited impatiently.

"He knows something that we don't," said Mr. Stobell, at last; "that's what it is."

Mr. Tredgold, who was too used to his friend's mental processes to quarrel with them, assented.

"He's coming round to smoke a pipe with me to-morrow night," he said, briskly, as he turned to cross the road to his office. "You come too, and we'll get it out of him. If Chalk can keep a secret he has altered, that's all I can say."

His estimate of Mr. Chalk proved correct. With Mr. Tredgold acting as cross-examining counsel and Mr. Stobell enacting the part of a partial and overbearing judge, Mr. Chalk, after a display of fortitude which surprised himself almost as much as it irritated his friends, parted with his news and sat smiling with gratification at their growing excitement.

"Half a million, and he won't go for it?" ejaculated Mr. Tredgold. "The man must be mad."

"No; he passed his word and he won't break it," said Mr. Chalk. "The captain's word is his bond, and I honour him for it. I can quite understand it."

Mr. Tredgold shrugged his shoulders and glanced at Mr. Stobell; that gentleman, after due deliberation, gave an assenting nod.

"He can't get at it, that's the long and short of it," said Mr. Tredgold, after a pause. "He had to leave it behind when he was rescued, or else risk losing it by telling the men who rescued him about it, and he's had no opportunity since. It wants money to take a ship out there and get it, and he doesn't see his way quite clear. He'll have it fast enough when he gets a chance. If not, why did he make that map?"

Mr. Chalk shook his head, and remarked mysteriously that the captain had his reasons. Mr. Tredgold relapsed into silence, and for some time the only sound audible came from a briar-pipe which Mr.

Stobell ought to have thrown away some years before.

"Have you given up that idea of a yachting cruise of yours, Chalk?" demanded Mr. Tredgold, turning on him suddenly.

"No," was the reply. "I was talking about it to Captain Bowers only the other day. That's how I got to hear of the treasure."

Mr. Tredgold started and gave a significant glance at Mr. Stobell. In return he got a wink which that gentleman kept for moments of mental confusion.

"What did the captain tell you for?" pursued Mr. Tredgold, returning to Mr. Chalk. "He wanted you to make an offer. He hasn't got the money for such an expedition; you have. The yarn about passing his word was so that you shouldn't open your mouth too wide. You were to do the persuading, and then he could make his own terms. Do you see? Why, it's as plain as A B C."

"Plain as the alphabet," said Mr. Stobell, almost chidingly.

Mr. Chalk gasped and looked from one to the other.

"I should like to have a chat with the captain about it," continued Mr. Tredgold, slowly and impressively. "I'm a business man and I could put it on a business footing. It's a big risk, of course; all those things are . . . but if we went shares . . . if we found the money——"

He broke off and, filling his pipe slowly, gazed in deep thought at the wall. His friends waited expectantly.

"Combine business with pleasure," resumed Mr. Tredgold, lighting his pipe; "sea-air . . . change . . . blow away the cobwebs . . . experience for Edward to be left alone. What do you think, Stobell?" he added, turning suddenly.

Mr. Stobell gripped the arms of his chair in his huge hands and drew his bulky figure to a more upright position.

"What do you mean by combining business with pleasure?" he said, eyeing him with dull suspicion.

"Chalk is set on a trip for the love of it," explained Mr. Tredgold.

"If we take on the contract, he ought to pay a bigger share, then," said the other, firmly.

"Perhaps he will," said Tredgold, hastily.

Mr. Stobell pondered again and, slightly raising one hand, indicated that he was in the throes of another idea and did not wish to be disturbed.

"You said it would be experience for Edward to be left alone," he said, accusingly.

"I did," was the reply.

"You ought to pay more, too, then," declared the contractor, "because it's serving of your ends as well."

"We can't split straws," exclaimed Tredgold, impatiently. "If the captain consents we three will find the money and divide our portion, whatever it is, equally."

Mr. Chalk, who had been in the clouds during this discussion, came back to earth again. "If he consents," he said, sadly; "but he won't."

"Well, he can only, refuse," said Mr. Tredgold; "and, anyway, we'll have the first refusal. Things like that soon get about. What do you say to a stroll? I can think better while I'm walking."

His friends assenting, they put on their hats and sallied forth. That they should stroll in the direction of Dialstone Lane surprised neither of them. Mr. Tredgold leading, they went round by the church, and that gentleman paused so long to admire the architecture that Mr. Stobell got restless.

"You've seen it before, Tredgold," he said, shortly.

"It's a fine old building," said the other. "Binchester ought to be proud of it. Why, here we are at Captain Bowers's!"

"The house has been next to the church for a couple o' hundred years," retorted his friend.

"Let's go in," said Mr. Tredgold. "Strike while the iron's hot. At any rate," he concluded, as Mr. Chalk voiced feeble objections, "we can see how the land lies."

He knocked at the door and then, stepping aside, left Mr. Chalk to lead the way in. Captain Bowers, who was sitting with Prudence, looked up at their entrance, and putting down his newspaper extended a hearty welcome.

"Chalk didn't like to pass without looking in," said Mr. Tredgold, "and I haven't seen you for some time. You know Stobell?"

The captain nodded, and Mr. Chalk, pale with excitement, accepted his accustomed pipe from the hands of Miss Drewitt and sat nervously awaiting events. Mr. Tasker set out the whisky, and, Miss Drewitt avowing a fondness for smoke in other people, a comfortable haze soon filled the room. Mr. Tredgold, with a significant glance at Mr. Chalk, said that it reminded him of a sea-fog.

It only reminded Mr. Chalk, however, of a smoky chimney from which he had once suffered, and he at once entered into minute details. The theme was an inspiriting one, and before Mr. Tredgold could hark back to the sea again Mr. Stobell was discoursing, almost eloquently for him, upon drains. From drains to the shortcomings of the district council they progressed by natural and easy stages, and it was not until Miss Drewitt had withdrawn to the clearer atmosphere above that a sudden ominous silence ensued, which Mr. Chalk saw clearly he was expected to break.

"I—I've been telling them some of your adventures," he said, desperately, as he glanced at the captain; "they're both interested in such things."

The latter gave a slight start and glanced shrewdly at his visitors. "Aye, aye," he said, composedly.

"Very interesting, some of them," murmured Mr. Tredgold. "I suppose you'll have another voyage or two before you've done? One, at any rate."

"No," said the captain, "I've had my share of the sea; other men may have a turn now. There's nothing to take me out again—nothing."

Mr. Tredgold coughed and murmured something about breaking off old habits too suddenly.

"It's a fine career," sighed Mr. Chalk.

"A manly life," said Mr. Tredgold, emphatically.

"It's like every other profession, it has two sides to it," said the captain.

"It is not so well paid as it should be," said the wily Tredgold, "but I suppose one gets chances of making money in outside ways sometimes."

The captain assented, and told of a steward of his who had made a small fortune by selling Japanese curios to people who didn't understand them.

The conversation was interesting, but extremely distasteful to a business man intent upon business. Mr. Stobell took his pipe out of his mouth and cleared his throat. "Why, you might build a hospital with it," he burst out, impatiently.

"Build a hospital!" repeated the astonished captain, as Mr. Chalk bent suddenly to do up his shoelace.

"Think of the orphans you could be a father to!" added Mr. Stobell, making the most of an unwonted fit of altruism.

The captain looked inquiringly at Mr. Tredgold.

"And widows," said Mr. Stobell, and, putting his pipe in his mouth as a sign that he had finished his remarks, gazed stolidly at the company.

"Stobell must be referring to a story Chalk told us of some precious stones you buried, I think," said Mr. Tredgold, reddening. "Aren't you, Stobell?"

"Of course I am," said his friend. "You know that."

Captain Bowers glanced at Mr. Chalk, but that gentleman was still busy with his shoe-lace, only looking up when Mr. Tredgold, taking the bull by the horns, made the captain a plain, straightforward offer to fit out and give him the command of an expedition to recover the treasure. In a speech which included the benevolent Mr. Stobell's hospitals, widows, and orphans, he pointed out a score of reasons why the captain should consent, and wound up with a glowing picture of Miss Drewitt as the heiress of the wealthiest man in Binchester. The captain heard him patiently to an end and then shook his head.

"I passed my word," he said, stiffly.

Mr. Stobell took his pipe out of his mouth again to offer a little encouragement. "Tredgold has broke his word before now," he observed; "he's got quite a name for it."

"But you would go out if it were not for that?" inquired Tredgold, turning a deaf ear to this remark.

"Naturally," said the captain, smiling; "but, then, you see I did."

Mr. Tredgold drummed with his fingers on the arms of his chair, and after a little hesitation asked as a great favour to be permitted to see the map. As an estate agent, he said, he took a professional interest in plans of all kinds.

Captain Bowers rose, and in the midst of an expectant silence took the map from the bureau, and placing it on the table kept it down with his fist. The others drew near and inspected it.

"Nobody but Captain Bowers has ever seen the other side," said Mr. Chalk, impressively.

"Except my niece," interposed the captain. "She wanted to see it, and I trust her as I would trust myself. She thinks the same as I do about it."

His stubby forefinger travelled slowly round the coast-line until, coming to the extreme south-west corner, it stopped, and a mischievous smile creased his beard.

"It's buried here," he observed. "All you've got to do is to find the island and dig in that spot."

Mr. Chalk laughed and shook his head as at a choice piece of waggishness.

"Suppose," said Mr. Tredgold, slowly—"suppose anybody found it without your connivance, would you take your share?"

"Let 'em find it first," said the captain.

"Yes, but would you?" inquired Mr. Chalk.

Captain Bowers took up the map and returned it to its place in the bureau. "You go and find it," he said, with a genial smile.

"You give us permission?" demanded Tredgold.

"Certainly," grinned the captain. "I give you permission to go and dig over all the islands in the Pacific; there's a goodish number of them, and it's a fairly common shape."

"It seems to me it's nobody's property," said Tredgold, slowly. "That is to say, it's anybody's that finds it. It isn't your property, Captain Bowers? You lay no claim to it?"

"No, no," said the captain. "It's nothing to do with me. You go and find it," he repeated, with enjoyment.

Mr. Tredgold laughed too, and his eye travelled mechanically towards the bureau. "If we do," he said, cordially, "you shall have your share."

The captain thanked him and, taking up the bottle, refilled their glasses. Then, catching the dull, brooding eye of Mr. Stobell as that plain-spoken man sat in a brown study trying to separate the serious from the jocular, he drank success to their search. He was about to give vent to further pleasantries when he was stopped by the mysterious behaviour of Mr. Chalk, who, first laying a finger on his lip to ensure silence, frowned severely and nodded at the door leading to the kitchen.

The other three looked in the direction indicated. The door stood half open, and the silhouette of a young woman in a large hat put the upper panels in shadow. The captain rose and, with a vigorous thrust of his foot, closed the door with a bang.

"Eavesdropping," said Mr. Chalk, in a tense whisper.

"There'll be a rival expedition," said the captain, falling in with his mood. "I've already warned that young woman off once. You'd better start tonight."

He leaned back in his chair and surveyed the company pleasantly. Somewhat to Mr. Chalk's disappointment Mr. Tredgold began to discuss agriculture, and they were still on that theme when they rose to depart some time later. Tredgold and Chalk bade the captain a cordial good-night; but Stobell, a creature of primitive impulses, found it difficult to shake hands with him. On the way home he expressed an ardent desire to tell the captain what men of sense thought of him.

The captain lit another pipe after they had gone, and for some time sat smoking and thinking over the events of the evening. Then Mr. Tasker's second infringement of discipline occurred to him, and, stretching out his hand, he rang the bell.

"Has that young woman gone?" he inquired, cautiously, as Mr. Tasker appeared.

"Yessir," was the reply.

"What about your articles?" demanded the captain, with sudden loudness. "What do you mean by it?"

Mr. Tasker eyed him forlornly. "It ain't my fault," he said, at last. "I don't want her."

"Eh?" said the other, sternly. "Don't talk nonsense. What do you have her here for, then?"

"Because I can't help myself," said Mr. Tasker, desperately; "that's why. She's took a fancy to me, and, that being so, it would take more than you and me to keep 'er away."

"Rubbish," said his master.

Mr. Tasker smiled wanly. "That's my reward for being steady," he said, with some bitterness; "that's what comes of having a good name in the place. I get Selina Vickers after me."

"You—you must have asked her to come here in the first place," said the astonished captain.

"Ask her?" repeated Mr. Tasker, with respectful scorn. "Ask her? She don't want no asking."

"What does she come for, then?" inquired the other.

"Me," said Mr. Tasker, brokenly. "I never dreamt o' such a thing. I was going 'er way one night—about three weeks ago, it was—and I walked with her as far as her road-Mint Street. Somehow it got put about that we were walking out. A week afterwards she saw me in Harris's, the grocer's, and waited outside for me till I come out and walked 'ome with me. After she came in the other night I found we was keeping company. To-night-tonight she got a ring out o' me, and now we're engaged."

"What on earth did you give her the ring for if you don't want her?" inquired the captain, eyeing him with genuine concern.

"Ah, it seems easy, sir," said the unfortunate; "but you don't know Selina. She bought the ring and said I was to pay it off a shilling a week. She took the first shilling to-night."

His master sat back and regarded him in amazement.

"You don't know Selina, sir," repeated Mr. Tasker, in reply to this manifestation. "She always gets her own way. Her father ain't 'it 'er mother not since Selina was seventeen. He dursent. The last time Selina went for him tooth and nail; smashed all the plates off the dresser throwing 'em at him, and ended by chasing of him up the road in his shirt-sleeves."

The captain grunted.

"That was two years ago," continued Mr. Tasker; "and his spirit's quite broke. He 'as to give all his money except a shilling a week to his wife, and he's not allowed to go into pubs. If he does it's no good, because they won't serve 'im. If they do Selina goes in next morning and gives them a piece of 'er mind. She don't care who's there or what she says, and the consequence is Mr. Vickers can't get served in Binchester for love or money. That'll show you what she is."

"Well, tell her I won't have her here," said the captain, rising. "Good-night."

"I've told her over and over again, sir," was the reply, "and all she says is she's not afraid of you, nor six like you."

The captain fell back silent, and Mr. Tasker, pausing in a respectful attitude, watched him wistfully. The captain's brows were bent in thought, and Mr. Tasker, reminding himself that crews had trembled at his nod and that all were silent when he spoke, felt a flutter of hope.

"Well," said the captain, sharply, as he turned and caught sight of him, "what are you waiting there for?"

Mr. Tasker drifted towards the door which led upstairs.

"I—I thought you were thinking of something we could do to prevent her coming, sir," he said, slowly. "It's hard on me, because as a matter of fact——"

"Well?" said the captain.

"I—I've 'ad my eye on another young lady for some time," concluded Mr. Tasker.

He was standing on the bottom stair as he spoke, with his hand on the latch. Under the baleful stare with which the indignant captain favoured him, he closed it softly and mounted heavily to bed.

CHAPTER V

Mr. Chalk's expedition to the Southern Seas became a standing joke with the captain, and he waylaid him on several occasions to inquire into the progress he was making, and to give him advice suitable for all known emergencies at sea, together with a few that are unknown. Even Mr. Chalk began to tire of his pleasantries, and, after listening to a surprising account of a Scotch vessel which always sailed backwards when the men whistled on Sundays, signified his displeasure by staying away from Dialstone Lane for some time.

Deprived of his society the captain consoled himself with that of Edward Tredgold, a young man for whom he was beginning to entertain a strong partiality, and whose observations of Binchester folk, flavoured with a touch of good-natured malice, were a source of never-failing interest.

"He is very wide-awake," he said to his niece. "There isn't much that escapes him."

Miss Drewitt, gazing idly out of window, said that she had not noticed it.

"Very clever at his business, I understand," said the captain.

His niece said that he had always appeared to her—when she had happened to give the matter a thought—as a picture of indolence.

"Ah! that's only his manner," replied the other, warmly. "He's a young man that's going to get on; he's going to make his mark. His father's got money, and he'll make more of it."

Something in the tone of his voice attracted his niece's attention, and she looked at him sharply as an almost incredible suspicion as to the motive of this conversation flashed on her.

"I don't like to see young men too fond of money," she observed, sedately.

"I didn't say that," said the captain, eagerly. "If anything, he is too open-handed. What I meant was that he isn't lazy."

"He seems to be very fond of coming to see you," said Prudence, by way of encouragement.

"Ah!" said the captain, "and—"

He stopped abruptly as the girl faced round. "And?" she prompted.

"And the crow's-nest," concluded the captain, somewhat lamely.

There was no longer room for doubt. Scarce two months ashore and he was trying his hand at matchmaking. Fresh from a world of obedient satellites, and ships responding to the lightest touch of the helm, he was venturing with all the confidence of ignorance upon the most delicate of human undertakings. Miss Drewitt, eyeing him with perfect comprehension and some little severity, sat aghast at his hardihood.

"He's very fond of going up there," said Captain Bowers, somewhat discomfited.

"Yes, he and Joseph have much in common," remarked Miss Drewitt, casually. "They're some what alike, too, I always fancy."

"Alike!" exclaimed the astonished captain.

"Edward Tredgold like Joseph? Why, you must be dreaming."

"Perhaps it's only my fancy," conceded Miss Drewitt, "but I always think that I can see a likeness."

"There isn't the slightest resemblance in the world," said the captain. "There isn't a single feature alike. Besides, haven't you ever noticed what a stupid expression Joseph has got?"

"Yes," said Miss Drewitt.

The captain scratched his ear and regarded her closely, but Miss Drewitt's face was statuesque in its repose.

"There—there's nothing wrong with your eyes, my dear?" he ventured, anxiously—"short sight or anything of that sort?"

"I don't think so," said his niece, gravely.

Captain Bowers shifted in his chair and, convinced that such a superficial observer must have overlooked many things, pointed out several admirable qualities in Edward Tredgold which he felt sure must have escaped her notice. The surprise with which Miss Drewitt greeted them all confirmed him in this opinion, and he was glad to think that he had called her attention to them ere it was too late.

"He's very popular in Binchester," he said, impressively. "Chalk told me that he is surprised he has not been married before now, seeing the way that he is run after."

"Dear me!" said his niece, with suppressed viciousness.

The captain smiled. He resolved to stand out for a long engagement when Mr. Tredgold came to him, and to stipulate also that they should not leave Binchester. An admirer in London to whom his niece had once or twice alluded—forgetting to mention that he was only ten—began to fade into what the captain considered proper obscurity.

Mr. Edward Tredgold reaped some of the benefits of this conversation when he called a day or two afterwards. The captain was out, but, encouraged by Mr. Tasker, who represented that his return might be looked for at any moment, he waited for over an hour, and was on the point of departure when Miss Drewitt entered.

"I should think that you must be tired of waiting?" she said, when he had explained.

"I was just going," said Mr. Tredgold, as he resumed his seat. "If you had been five minutes later you would have found an empty chair. I suppose Captain Bowers won't be long now?"

"He might be," said the girl.

"I'll give him a little while longer if I may," said Mr. Tredgold. "I'm very glad now that I waited—very glad indeed."

There was so much meaning in his voice that Miss Drewitt felt compelled to ask the reason.

"Because I was tired when I came in and the rest has done me good," explained Mr. Tredgold, with much simplicity. "Do you know that I sometimes think I work too hard?"

Miss Drewitt raised her eyebrows slightly and said, "Indeed!—I am very glad that you are rested," she added, after a pause.

"Thank you," said Mr. Tredgold, gratefully. "I came to see the captain about a card-table I've discovered for him. It's a Queen Anne, I believe; one of the best things I've ever seen. It's poked away in the back room of a cottage, and I only discovered it by accident."

"It's very kind of you," said Miss Drewitt, coldly, "but I don't think that my uncle wants any more furniture; the room is pretty full now."

"I was thinking of it for your room," said Mr. Tredgold.

"Thank you, but my room is full," said the girl, sharply.

"It would go in that odd little recess by the fireplace," continued the unmoved Mr. Tredgold. "We tried to get a small table for it before you came, but we couldn't see anything we fancied. I promised the captain I'd keep my eyes open for something."

Miss Drewitt looked at him with growing indignation, and wondered whether Mr. Chalk had added her to his list of the victims of Mr. Tredgold's blandishments.

"Why not buy it for yourself?" she demanded.

"No money," said Mr. Tredgold, shaking his head. "You forget that I lost two pounds to Chalk the other day, owing to your efforts."

"Well, I don't wish for it," said Miss Drewitt, firmly. "Please don't say anything to my uncle about it."

Mr. Tredgold looked disappointed. "As you please, of course," he remarked.

"Old things always seem a little bit musty," said the girl, softening a little. "I, should think that I saw the ghosts of dead and gone players sitting round the table. I remember reading a story about that once."

"Well, what about the other things?" said Mr. Tredgold. "Look at those old chairs, full of ghosts sitting piled up in each other's laps—there's no reason why you should only see one sitter at a time. Think of that beautifully-carved four-poster."

"My uncle bought that," said Miss Drewitt, somewhat irrelevantly.

"Yes, but I got it for him," said Mr. Tredgold. "You can't pick up a thing like that at a moment's notice—I had my eye on it for years; all the time old Brown was bedridden, in fact. I used to go and see him and take him tobacco, and he promised me that I should have it when he had done with it."

"Done with it?" repeated the girl, in a startled voice. "Did—did he get another one, then?"

Mr. Tredgold, roused from the pleasurable reminiscences of a collector, remembered himself suddenly. "Oh, yes, he got another one," he said, soothingly.

"Is—is he bedridden now?" inquired the girl.

"I haven't seen him for some time," said Mr. Tredgold, truthfully. "He gave up smoking and—and then I didn't go to see him, you know."

"He's dead," said Miss Drewitt, shivering. "He died in — Oh, you are horrible!"

"That carving—" began Mr. Tredgold.

"Don't talk about it, please," said the indignant Miss Drewitt. "I can't understand why my uncle should have listened to your advice at all; you must have forced it on him. I'm sure he didn't know how you got it."

"Yes, he did," said the other. "In fact, it was intended for his room at first. He was quite pleased with it."

"Why did he alter his mind, then?" inquired the girl.

Mr. Tredgold looked suddenly at the opposite wall, but his lips quivered and his eyes watered. Miss Drewitt, reading these signs aright, was justly incensed.

"I don't believe it," she cried.

"He said that you didn't know and he did," said Mr. Tredgold, apologetically. "I talk too much. I'd no business to let out about old Brown, but I forgot for the moment—sailors are always prone to childish superstitions."

"Are you talking about my uncle?" inquired Miss Drewitt, with ominous calm.

"They were his own words," said the other.

Miss Drewitt, feeling herself baffled, sat for some time wondering how to find fault politely with the young man before her. Her mind was full of subject-matter, but the politeness easily eluded her. She threw out after a time the suggestion that his presence at the bedside of sick people was not likely to add to their comfort.

Captain Bowers entered before the aggrieved Mr. Tredgold could think of a fitting reply, and after a hasty greeting insisted upon his staying for a cup of tea. By a glance in the visitor's direction and a faint smile Miss Drewitt was understood to endorse the invitation.

The captain's satisfaction at finding them together was complete, but a little misunderstanding was caused all round, when Mr. Tasker came in with the tea, by the series of nods and blinks by which the captain strove to call his niece's attention to various facial and other differences between his servant and their visitor. Mr. Tredgold, after standing it for some time, created a little consternation by inquiring whether he had got a smut on his nose.

The captain was practically the only talker at tea, but the presence of two attentive listeners prevented him from discovering the fact. He described his afternoon's ramble at such length that it was getting late by the time they had finished.

"Stay and smoke a pipe," he said, as he sought his accustomed chair.

Mr. Tredgold assented in the usual manner by saying that he ought to be going, and instead of one pipe smoked three or four. The light failed and the lamp was lit, but he still stayed on until the sound of subdued but argumentative voices beyond the drawn blind apprised them of other visitors. The thin tones of Mr. Chalk came through the open window, apparently engaged in argument with a bear. A faint sound of hustling and growling, followed by a gentle bumping against the door, seemed to indicate that he—or perhaps the bear—was having recourse to physical force.

"Come in," cried the captain.

The door opened and Mr. Chalk, somewhat flushed, entered, leading Mr. Stobell. The latter gentleman seemed in a surly and reluctant frame of mind, and having exchanged greetings subsided silently into a chair and sat eyeing Mr. Chalk, who, somewhat nervous as to his reception after so long an absence, plunged at once into conversation.

"I thought I should find you here," he said, pleasantly, to Edward Tredgold.

"Why?" demanded Mr. Tredgold, with what Mr. Chalk thought unnecessary abruptness.

"Well—well, because you generally are here, I suppose," he said, somewhat taken aback.

Mr. Tredgold favoured him with a scowl, and a somewhat uncomfortable silence ensued.

"Stobell wanted to see you again," said Mr. Chalk, turning to the captain. "He's done nothing but talk about you ever since he was here last."

Captain Bowers said he was glad to see him; Mr. Stobell returned the courtesy with an odd noise in his throat and a strange glare at Mr. Chalk.

"I met him to-night," continued that gentleman, "and nothing would do for him but to come on here."

It was evident from the laboured respiration of the ardent Mr. Stobell, coupled with a word or two which had filtered through the window, that the ingenious Mr. Chalk was using him as a stalking-horse. From the fact that Mr. Stobell made no denial it was none the less evident, despite the growing blackness of his appearance, that he was a party to the arrangement. The captain began to see the reason.

"It's all about that island," explained Mr. Chalk; "he can talk of nothing else."

The captain suppressed a groan, and Mr. Tredgold endeavoured, but without success, to exchange smiles with Miss Drewitt.

"Aye, aye," said the captain, desperately.

"He's as eager as a child that's going to its first pantomime," continued Mr. Chalk.

Mr. Stobell's appearance was so alarming that he broke off and eyed him with growing uneasiness.

"You were talking about a pantomime," said Mr. Tredgold, after a long pause.

Mr. Chalk cast an imploring glance at Mr. Stobell to remind him of their compact, and resumed.

"Talks of nothing else," he said, watching his friend, "and can't sleep for thinking of it."

"That's bad," said Mr. Tredgold, sympathetically. "Has he tried shutting his eyes and counting sheep jumping over a stile?"

"No, he ain't," said Mr. Stobell, exploding suddenly, and turning a threatening glance on the speaker. "And what's more," he added, in more ordinary tones, "he ain't going to."

"We—we've been thinking of that trip again," interposed Mr. Chalk, hurriedly. "The more Stobell thinks of it the more he likes it. You know what you said the last time we were here?"

The captain wrinkled his brows and looked at him inquiringly.

"Told us to go and find the island," Mr. Chalk reminded him. "You said, 'I've shown you a map of the island; now go and find it.'"

"Oh, aye," said the captain, with a laugh, "so I did."

"Stobell was wondering," continued Mr. Chalk, "whether you couldn't give us just a little bit more of a hint, without breaking your word, of course."

"I don't see how it could be done, "replied the captain, pondering; "a promise is a promise."

Mr. Chalk's face fell. He moved his chair aside mechanically to make room for Mr. Tasker, who had entered with a tray and glasses, and sat staring at the floor. Then he raised his eyes and met a significant glance from Mr. Stobell.

"I suppose we may have another look at the map?" he said, softly; "just a glance to freshen our memories."

The captain, who had drawn his chair to the table to preside over the tray, looked up impatiently.

"No," he said, brusquely.

Mr. Chalk looked hurt. "I'm very sorry," he said, in surprise at the captain's tone. "You showed it to us the other day, and I didn't think—"

"The fact is," said the captain, in a more gentle voice—"the fact is, I can't."

"Can't?" repeated the other.

"It is not very pleasant to keep on refusing friends," said the captain, making amends for his harshness by pouring a serious overdose of whisky into Mr. Chalk's glass, "and it's only natural for you to be anxious about it, so I removed the temptation out of my way."

"Removed the temptation?" repeated Mr. Chalk.

"I burnt the map," said the captain, with a smile.

"Burnt it?" gasped Mr. Chalk. "BURNT it?"

"Burnt it to ashes," said the captain, jovially.

"It's a load off my mind. I ought to have done it before. In fact, I never ought to have made the map at all."

Mr. Chalk stared at him in speechless dismay.

"Try that," said the captain, handing Mr. Stobell his glass.

Mr. Stobell took it from mere force of habit, and sat holding it in his hand as though he had forgotten what to do with it.

"I did it yesterday morning," said the captain, noticing their consternation. "I had just lit my pipe after breakfast, and I suppose the match put me in mind of it. I took out the map and set light to it at Cape Silvio. The flame ran half-way round the coast and then popped through the middle of the paper and converted Mount Lonesome into a volcano."

He gave a boisterous laugh and, raising his glass, nodded to Mr. Stobell. Mr. Stobell, who was just about to drink, lowered his glass again and frowned.

"I don't see anything to laugh at," he said, deliberately.

"He can't have been listening," said Mr. Tredgold, in a low voice, to Miss Drewitt.

"Well, it's done now," said the captain, genially. "You—you're not going?"

"Yes, I am," said Mr. Stobell.

He bade them good-night, and then pausing at the door stood and surveyed them; even Mr. Tasker, who was gliding in unobtrusively with a jug of water, shared in his regards.

"When I think of the orphans and widows," he said, bitterly, "I——"

He opened the door suddenly and, closing it behind him, breathed the rest to Dialstone Lane. An aged woman sitting in a doorway said, "*Hush!*"

CHAPTER VI

Miss Drewitt sat for some time in her room after the visitors had departed, eyeing with some disfavour the genuine antiques which she owed to the enterprise, not to say officiousness, of Edward Tredgold. That they were in excellent taste was undeniable, but there was a flavour of age and a suspicion of decay about them which did not make for cheerfulness.

She rose at last, and taking off her watch went through the nightly task of wondering where she had put the key after using it last. It was not until she had twice made a fruitless tour of the room with the candle that she remembered that she had left it on the mantelpiece downstairs.

The captain was still below, and after a moment's hesitation she opened her door and went softly down the steep winding stairs.

The door at the foot stood open, and revealed the captain standing by the table. There was an air of perplexity and anxiety about him such as she had never seen before, and as she waited he crossed to the bureau, which stood open, and searched feverishly among the papers which littered it. Apparently dissatisfied with the result, he moved it out bodily and looked behind and beneath it. Coming to an erect position again he suddenly became aware of the presence of his niece.

"It's gone," he said, in an amazed voice.

"Gone?" repeated Prudence. "What has gone?"

"The map," said the captain, tumbling his beard. "I put it in this end pigeon-hole the other night after showing it and I haven't touched it since; and it's gone."

"But you burnt it!" said Prudence, with an astonished laugh.

The captain started. "No; I was going to," he said, eyeing her in manifest confusion.

"But you said that you had," persisted his niece.

"Yes," stammered the captain, "I know I did, but I hadn't. I was just looking ahead a bit, that was all. I went to the bureau just now to do it."

Miss Drewitt eyed him with mild reproach. "You even described how you did it," she said, slowly. "You said that Mount Lonesome turned into a volcano. Wasn't it true?"

"Figure o' speech, my dear," said the unhappy captain; "I've got a talent for description that runs away with me at times."

His niece gazed at him in perplexity.

"You know what Chalk is," said Captain Bowers, appealingly. "I was going to do it yesterday, only I forgot it, and he would have gone down on his knees for another sight of it. I don't like to seem disobliging to friends, and it seemed to me a good way out of it. Chalk is so eager— it's like refusing a child, and I hurt his feelings only the other day."

"Perhaps you burnt it after all and forgot it?" said Prudence.

For the first time in her knowledge of him the captain got irritable with her. "I've not burnt it," he said, sharply. "Where's that Joseph? He must know something about it!"

He moved to the foot of the staircase, but Miss Drewitt laid a detaining hand on his arm.

"Joseph was in the room when you said that you had burnt it," she exclaimed. "You can't contradict yourself like that before him. Besides, I'm sure he has had nothing to do with it."

"Somebody's got it," grumbled her uncle, pausing.

He dropped into his chair and looked at her in consternation. "Good heavens! Suppose they go after it," he said, in a choking voice.

"Well, it won't be your fault," said Prudence. "You haven't broken your word intentionally."

But the captain paid no heed. He was staring wild-eyed into vacancy and rumpling his grey hair until it stood at all angles. His face reflected varying emotions.

"Somebody has got it," he said again.

"Whoever it is will get no good by it," said Miss Drewitt, who had had a pious upbringing.

"And if they've got the map they'll go after the island," said the captain, pursuing his train of thought.

"Perhaps they won't find it after all," said Prudence.

"Perhaps they won't," said the captain, gruffly.

He got up and paced the room restlessly. Prudence, watching him with much sympathy, had a sudden idea.

"Edward Tredgold was in here alone this afternoon," she said, significantly.

"No, no," said the captain, warmly. "Whoever has got it, it isn't Edward Tredgold. I expect the talk about it has leaked out and somebody has slipped in and taken it. I ought to have been more careful."

"He started when you said that you had burnt it," persisted Miss Drewitt, unwilling to give up a theory so much to her liking. "You mark my words if his father and Mr. Chalk and that Mr. Stobell don't go away for a holiday soon. Good-night."

She kissed him affectionately under the left eye—a place overlooked by his beard—and went upstairs again. The captain filled his pipe and, resuming his chair, sat in a brown study until the clock of the neighbouring church struck two.

It was about the same time that Mr. Chalk fell asleep, thoroughly worn out by the events of the evening and a conversation with Mr. Stobell and Mr. Tredgold, whom he had met on the way home waiting for him.

The opinion of Mr. Tredgold senior, an opinion in which Mr. Stobell fully acquiesced, was that Mr. Chalk had ruined everything by displaying all along a youthful impetuosity sadly out of place in one of his years and standing. The offender's plea that he had thought it best to strike while the iron was hot only exposed him to further contumely.

"Well, it's no good talking about it," said Mr. Tredgold, impatiently. "It's all over now and done with."

"Half a million clean chucked away," said Mr. Stobell.

Mr. Chalk shook his head and, finding that his friends had by no means exhausted the subject, suddenly bethought himself of an engagement and left them.

Miss Vickers, who heard the news from Mr. Joseph Tasker, received it with an amount of amazement highly gratifying to his powers as a narrator. Her strongly expressed opinion afterwards that he had misunderstood what he had heard was not so agreeable.

"I suppose I can believe my own ears?" he said, in an injured voice.

"He must have been making fun of them all," said Selina. "He couldn't have burnt it—he couldn't."

"Why not?" inquired the other, surprised at her vehemence.

Miss Vickers hesitated. "Because it would be such a silly thing to do," she said, at last. "Now, tell me what you heard all over again—slow."

Mr. Tasker complied.

"I can't make head or tail of it," said Miss Vickers when he had finished.

"Seems simple enough to me," said Joseph, staring at her.

"All things seem simple when you don't know them," said Miss Vickers, vaguely.

She walked home in a thoughtful mood, and for a day or two went about the house with an air of preoccupation which was a source of much speculation to the family. George Vickers, aged six, was driven to the verge of madness by being washed. Three times in succession one morning; a gag of well-soaped flannel being applied with mechanical regularity each time that he strove to point out the unwashed condition of Martha and Charles. His turn came when the exultant couple, charged with having made themselves dirty in the shortest time on record, were deprived of their breakfast. Mr. Vickers, having committed one or two minor misdemeanours unchallenged, attributed his daughter's condition to love, and began to speak of that passion with more indulgence than he had done since his marriage.

Miss Vickers's' abstraction, however, lasted but three days. On the fourth she was herself again, and, having spent the day in hard work, dressed herself with unusual care in the evening and went out.

The evening was fine and the air, to one who had been at work indoors all day, delightful. Miss Vickers walked briskly along with the smile of a person who has solved a difficult problem, but as she drew near the Horse and Groom, a hostelry of retiring habits, standing well back from the road, the smile faded and she stood face to face with the stern realities of life.

A few yards from the side-door Mr. Vickers stood smoking a contemplative pipe; the side-door itself had just closed behind a tall man in corduroys, who bore in his right hand a large mug made of pewter.

"Ho!" said Selina, "so this is how you go on the moment my back is turned, is it?"

"What d'ye mean?" demanded Mr. Vickers, blustering.

"You know what I mean," said his daughter, "standing outside and sending Bill Russell in to get you beer. That's what I mean."

Mr. Vickers turned, and with a little dramatic start intimated that he had caught sight of Mr. Russell for the first time that evening. Mr. Russell himself sought to improve the occasion.

"Wish I may die—" he began, solemnly.

"Like a policeman," continued Selina, regarding her father indignantly.

"I wish I *was* a policeman," muttered Mr. Vickers. "I'd show some of you."

"What have you got to say for yourself?" demanded Miss Vickers, shortly.

"Nothing," said the culprit. "I s'pose I can stand where I like? There's no law agin it."

"Do you mean to say that you didn't send Bill in to get you some beer?" said his daughter.

"Certainly not," said Mr. Vickers, with great indignation. "I shouldn't think of such a thing."

"I shouldn't get it if 'e did," said Mr. Russell, virtuously.

"Whose beer is it, then?" said Selina.

"Why, Bill's, I s'pose; how should I know?" replied Mr. Vickers.

"Yes, it's mine," said Mr. Russell.

"Drink it up, then," commanded Miss Vickers, sternly.

Both men started, and then Mr. Russell, bestowing a look of infinite compassion upon his unfortunate friend, raised the mug obediently to his sensitive lips. Always a kind-hearted man, he was glad when the gradual tilting necessary to the occasion had blotted out the picture of indignation which raged helplessly before him.

"I 'ope you're satisfied now," he said severely to the girl, as he turned a triumphant glance on Mr. Vickers, which that gentleman met with a cold stare.

Miss Vickers paid no heed. "You get off home," she said to her father; "I'll see to the Horse and Groom to-morrow."

Mr. Vickers muttered something under his breath, and then, with a forlorn attempt at dignity, departed.

Miss Vickers, ignoring the remarks of one or two fathers of families who were volunteering information as to what they would do if she were their daughter, watched him out of sight and resumed her walk. She turned once or twice as though to make sure that she was not observed, and then, making her way in the direction of Mr. Chalk's house, approached it cautiously from the back.

Mr. Chalk, who was in the garden engaged in the useful and healthful occupation of digging, became aware after a time of a low whistle proceeding from the farther end. He glanced almost mechanically in that direction, and then nearly dropped his spade as he made out a girl's head surmounted by a large hat. The light was getting dim, but the hat had an odd appearance of familiarity. A stealthy glance in the other direction showed him the figure of Mrs. Chalk standing to attention just inside the open French windows of the drawing-room.

The whistle came again, slightly increased in volume. Mr. Chalk, pausing merely to wipe his brow, which had suddenly become very damp, bent to his work with renewed vigour. It is an old idea that whistling aids manual labour; Mr. Chalk, moistening his lips with a tongue grown all too feverish for the task, began to whistle a popular air with much liveliness.

The idea was ingenious, but hopeless from the start. The whistle at the end of the garden became piercing in its endeavour to attract attention, and, what was worse, developed an odd note of entreaty. Mr. Chalk, pale with apprehension, could bear no more.

"Well, I think I've done enough for one night," he observed, cheerfully and loudly, as he thrust his spade into the ground and took his coat from a neighbouring bush.

He turned to go indoors and, knowing his wife's objection to dirty boots, made for the door near the kitchen. As he passed the drawing-room window, however, a low but imperative voice pronounced his name.

"Yes, my dear," said Mr. Chalk.

"There's a friend of yours whistling for you," said his wife, with forced calmness.

"Whistling?" said Mr. Chalk, with as much surprise as a man could assume in face of the noise from the bottom of the garden.

"Do you mean to tell me you can't hear it?" demanded his wife, in a choking voice.

Mr. Chalk lost his presence of mind. "I thought it was a bird," he said, assuming a listening attitude.

"*Bird?*" gasped the indignant Mrs. Chalk. "Look down there. Do you call that a bird?"

Mr. Chalk looked and uttered a little cry of astonishment.

"I suppose she wants to see one of the servants," he said, at last; "but why doesn't she go round to the side entrance? I shall have to speak to them about it."

Mrs. Chalk drew herself up and eyed him with superb disdain.

"Go down and speak to her," she commanded. "Certainly not," said Mr. Chalk, braving her, although his voice trembled.

"Why not?"

"Because if I did you would ask me what she said, and when I told you you wouldn't believe me," said Mr. Chalk.

"You—you decline to go down?" said his wife, in a voice shaking with emotion.

"I do," said Mr. Chalk, firmly. "Why don't you go yourself?"

Mrs. Chalk eyed him for a moment in scornful silence, and then stepped to the window and sailed majestically down the garden. Mr. Chalk watched her, with parted lips, and then he began to breathe more freely as the whistle ceased and the head suddenly disappeared. Still a little nervous, he watched his wife to the end of the garden and saw her crane her head over the fence. By the time she returned he was sitting in an attitude of careless ease, with his back to the window.

"Well?" he said, with assurance.

Mrs. Chalk stood stock-still, and the intensity of her gaze drew Mr. Chalk's eyes to her face despite his will. For a few seconds she gazed at him in silence, and then, drawing her skirts together, swept violently out of the room.

CHAPTER VII

Mr. Chalk made but a poor breakfast next morning, the effort to display a feeling of proper sympathy with Mrs. Chalk, who was presiding in gloomy silence at the coffee-pot, and at the same time to maintain an air of cheerful innocence as to the cause of her behaviour, being almost beyond his powers. He chipped his egg with a painstaking attempt to avoid noise, and swallowed each mouthful with a feeble pretence of not knowing that she was watching him as he ate. Her glance conveyed a scornful reproach that he could eat at all in such circumstances, and, that there might be no mistake as to her own feelings, she ostentatiously pushed the toast-rack and egg-stand away from her.

"You—you're not eating, my dear," said Mr. Chalk.

"If I ate anything it would choke me," was the reply.

Mr. Chalk affected surprise, but his voice quavered. To cover his discomfiture he passed his cup up for more coffee, shivering despite himself, as he noticed the elaborate care which Mrs. Chalk displayed in rinsing out the cup and filling it to the very brim. Beyond raising her eyes to the ceiling when he took another piece of toast, she made no sign.

"You're not looking yourself," ventured Mr. Chalk, after a time.

His wife received the information silence.

"I've noticed it for some time," said the thoughtful husband, making another effort. "It's worried me."

"I'm not getting younger, I know," assented Mrs. Chalk. "But if you think that that's any excuse for your goings on, you're mistaken."

Mr. Chalk murmured something to the effect that he did not understand her.

"You understand well enough," was the reply. "When that girl came whistling over the fence last night you said you thought it was a bird."

"I did," said Mr. Chalk, hastily taking a spoonful of egg.

Mrs. Chalk's face flamed. "What sort of bird?" she demanded.

"Singin' bird," replied her husband, with nervous glibness.

Mrs. Chalk left the room.

Mr. Chalk finished his breakfast with an effort, and then, moving to the window, lit his pipe and sat for some time in moody thought. A little natural curiosity as to the identity of the fair whistler would, however, not be denied, and the names of Binchester's fairest daughters passed in review before him. Almost unconsciously he got up and surveyed himself in the glass.

"There's no accounting for tastes," he said to himself, in modest explanation.

His mind still dwelt on the subject as he stood in the hall later on in the morning, brushing his hat, preparatory to taking his usual walk. Mrs. Chalk, upstairs listening, thought that he would never have finished, and drew her own conclusions.

With the air of a man whose time hangs upon his hands Mr. Chalk sauntered slowly through the narrow by-ways of Binchester. He read all the notices pasted on the door of the Town Hall and bought some stamps at the post-office, but the morning dragged slowly, and he bent his steps at last in the direction of Tredgold's office, in the faint hope of a little conversation.

To his surprise, Mr. Tredgold senior was in an unusually affable mood. He pushed his papers aside at once, and, motioning his visitor to a chair, greeted him with much heartiness.

"Just the man I wanted to see," he said, cheerfully. "I want you to come round to my place at eight o'clock to-night. I've just seen Stobell, and he's coming too."

"I will if I can," said Mr. Chalk.

"You must come," said the other, seriously. "It's business."

"Business!" said Mr. Chalk. "I don't see—"

"You will to-night," said Mr. Tredgold, with a mysterious smile. "I've sent Edward off to town on business, and we sha'n't be interrupted. Goodbye. I'm busy."

He shook hands with his visitor and led him to the door; Chalk, after a vain attempt to obtain particulars, walked slowly home.

Despite his curiosity it was nearly half-past eight when he arrived at Mr. Tredgold's that evening, and was admitted by his host. The latter, with a somewhat trite remark about the virtues of punctuality, led the way upstairs and threw open the door of his study.

"Here he is," he announced.

A slender figure sitting bolt upright in a large grandfather-chair turned at their entrance, and revealed to the astonished Mr. Chalk the expressive features of Miss Selina Vickers; facing her at the opposite side of the room Mr. Stobell, palpably ruffled, eyed her balefully.

"This is a new client of mine," said Tredgold, indicating Miss Vickers.

Mr. Chalk said "Good evening."

"I tried to get a word with you last night," said Miss Vickers. "I was down at the bottom of your garden whistling for over ten minutes as hard as I could whistle. I wonder you didn't hear me."

"Hear you!" cried Mr. Chalk, guiltily conscious of a feeling of disappointment quite beyond his control.

"What do you mean by coming and whistling for me, eh? What do you mean by it?"

"I wanted to see you private," said Miss Vickers, calmly, "but it's just as well. I went and saw Mr. Tredgold this morning instead."

"On a matter of business," said Mr. Tredgold, looking at her. "She came to me, as one of the ordinary public, about some—ha—land she's interested in."

"An island," corroborated Miss Vickers.

Mr. Chalk took a chair and looked round in amazement. "What, another?" he said, faintly.

Mr. Tredgold coughed. "My client is not a rich woman," he began.

"Chalk knows that," interrupted Mr. Stobell. "The airs and graces that girl will give herself if you go on like that—"

"But she has some property there which she is anxious to obtain," continued Mr. Tredgold, with a warning glance at the speaker. "That being so—"

"Make him wish he may die first," interposed Miss Vickers, briskly.

"Yes, yes; that's all right," said Tredgold, meeting Mr. Chalk's startled gaze.

"It will be when he's done it," retorted the determined Miss Vickers.

"It's a secret," explained Mr. Tredgold, addressing his staring friend. "And you must swear to keep it if it's told you. That's what she means. I've had to and so has Stobell."

A fierce grunt from Mr. Stobell, who was still suffering from the remembrance of an indignity against which he had protested in vain, came as confirmation. Then the marvelling Mr. Chalk rose, and instructed by Miss Vickers took an oath, the efficacy of which consisted in a fervent hope that he might die if he broke it.

"But what's it all about?" he inquired, plaintively.

Mr. Tredgold conferred with Miss Vickers, and that lady, after a moment's hesitation, drew a folded paper from her bosom and beckoned to Mr. Chalk. With a cry of amazement he recognised the identical map of Bowers's Island, which he had last seen in the hands of its namesake. It was impossible to mistake it, although an attempt to take it in his hand was promptly frustrated by the owner.

"But Captain Bowers said that he had burnt it," he cried.

Mr. Tredgold eyed him coldly. "Burnt what?" he inquired.

"The map," was the reply.

"Just so," said Tredgold. "You told me he had burnt a map."

"Is this another, then?" inquired Mr. Chalk.

"P'r'aps," said Miss Vickers, briefly.

"As the captain said he had burnt his, this must be another," said Tredgold.

"Didn't he burn it, then?" inquired Mr. Chalk.

"I should be sorry to disbelieve Captain Bowers," said Tredgold.

"Couldn't be done," said the brooding Stobell, "not if you tried."

Mr. Chalk sat still and eyed them in perplexity.

"There is no doubt that this map refers to the same treasure as the one Captain Bowers had," said Tredgold, with the air of one making a generous admission. "My client has not volunteered any statement as to how it came into her possession—"

"And she's not going to," put in Miss Vickers, dispassionately.

"It is enough for me that we have got it," resumed Mr. Tredgold. "Now, we want you to join us in fitting out a ship and recovering the treasure. Equal expenses; equal shares."

"What about Captain Bowers?" inquired Mr. Chalk.

"He is to have an equal share without any of the expense," said Tredgold. "You know he gave us permission to find it if we could, so we are not injuring anybody."

"He told us to go and find it, if you remember," said Stobell, "and we're going to."

"He'll have a fortune handed to him without any trouble or being responsible in any way," said Tredgold, impressively. "I should like to think there was somebody working to put a fortune like that into my lap. We shall have a fifth each."

"That'll be five-thousand-pounds for you, Selina," said Mr. Stobell, with a would-be benevolent smile.

Miss Vickers turned a composed little face upon him and languidly closed one eye.

"I had two prizes for arithmetic when I was at school," she remarked; "and don't you call me Selina, unless you want to be called Bobbie."

A sharp exclamation from Mr. Tredgold stopped all but the first three words of Mr. Stobell's retort, but he said the rest under his breath with considerable relish.

"Don't mind him," said Miss Vickers. "I'm half sorry I let him join, now. A man that used to work for him once told me that he was only half a gentleman, but he'd never seen that half."

Mr. Stobell, afraid to trust himself, got up and leaned out of the window.

"Well, we're all agreed, then," said Tredgold, looking round.

"Half a second," said Miss Vickers. "Before I part with this map you've all got to sign a paper promising me my proper share, and to give me twenty pounds down."

Mr. Tredgold hesitated and looked serious. Mr. Chalk, somewhat dazed by the events of the evening, blinked at him solemnly. Mr. Stobell withdrew his head from the window and spoke.

"TWENTY-POUNDS!" he growled.

"Twenty pounds," repeated Miss Vickers, "or four hundred shillings, if you like it better. If you wait a moment I'll make it pennies."

She leaned back in her chair and, screwing her eyes tight, began the calculation. "Twelve noughts are nought," she said, in a gabbling whisper; "twelve noughts are nought, twelve fours are forty—"

"All right," said Mr. Tredgold, who had been regarding this performance with astonished disapproval. "You shall have the twenty pounds, but there is no necessity for us to sign any paper."

"No, there's no necessity," said Miss Vickers, opening her small, sharp eyes again, "only, if you don't do it, I'll find somebody that will."

Mr. Tredgold argued with her, but in vain; Mr. Chalk, taking up the argument and expanding it, fared no better; and Mr. Stobell, opening his mouth to contribute his mite, was quelled before he could get a word out.

"Them's my terms," said Miss Vickers; "take'em or leave'em, just as you please. I give you five minutes by the clock to make up your minds; Mr. Stobell can have six, because thinking takes him longer. And if you agree to do what's right—and I'm letting you off easy—Mr. Tredgold is to keep the map and never to let it go out of his sight for a single instant."

She put her head round the side of the chair to make a note of the time, and then, sitting upright with her arms folded, awaited their decision. Before the time was up the terms were accepted, and Mr. Tredgold, drawing his chair to the table, prepared to draw up the required agreement.

He composed several, but none which seemed to give general satisfaction. At the seventh attempt, however, he produced an agreement which, alluding in vague terms to a treasure quest in the Southern Seas on the strength of a map provided by Miss Vickers, promised one-fifth of the sum recovered to that lady, and was considered to meet the exigencies of the case. Miss Vickers herself, without being enthusiastic, said that she supposed it would have to do.

Another copy was avoided, but only with great difficulty, owing to her criticism of Mr. Stobell's signature. It took the united and verbose efforts of Messrs. Chalk and Tredgold to assure her that it was in his usual style, and rather a good signature for him than otherwise. Miss Vickers, viewing it with her head on one side, asked whether he couldn't make his mark instead; a question which Mr. Stobell, at the pressing instance of his friends, left unanswered. Then Tredgold left the room to pay a visit to his safe, and, the other two gentlemen turning out their pockets, the required sum was made up, and with the agreement handed to Miss Vickers in exchange for the map.

She bade them good-night, and then, opening the door, paused with her hand on the knob and stood irresolute.

"I hope I've done right," she said, somewhat nervously. "It was no good to anybody laying idle and being wasted. I haven't stolen anything."

"No, no," said Tredgold, hastily.

"It seems ridiculous for all that money to be wasted," continued Miss Vickers, musingly. "It doesn't belong to anybody, so nobody can be hurt by our taking it, and we can do a lot of good with it, if we like. I shall give some of mine away to the poor. We all will. I'll have it put in this paper."

She fumbled in her bodice for the document, and walked towards them.

"We can't alter it now," said Mr. Tredgold, decidedly.

"We'll do what's right," said Mr. Chalk, reassuringly.

Miss Vickers smiled at him. "Yes, I know you will," she said, graciously, "and I think Mr. Tredgold will, but—"

"You're leaving that door open," said Mr. Stobell, coldly, "and the draught's blowing my head off, pretty near."

Miss Vickers eyed him scornfully, but in the absence of a crushing reply disdained one at all. She contented herself instead by going outside and closing the door after her with a sharpness which stirred every hair on his head.

"It's a most extraordinary thing," said Mr. Chalk, as the three bent exultingly over the map. "I could ha' sworn to this map in a court of justice."

"Don't you worry your head about it," advised Mr. Stobell.

"You've got your way at last," said Tredgold, with some severity. "We're going for a cruise with you, and here you are raising objections."

"Not objections," remonstrated the other; "and, talking about the voyage, what about Mrs. Chalk? She'll want to come."

"So will Mrs. Stobell," said that lady's proprietor, "but she won't."

"She mustn't hear of it till the last moment," said Tredgold, dictatorially; "the quieter we keep the whole thing the better. You're not to divulge a word of the cruise to anybody. When it does leak out it must be understood we are just going for a little pleasure jaunt. Mind, you've sworn to keep the whole affair secret."

Mr. Chalk screwed up his features in anxious perplexity, but made no comment.

"The weather's fine," continued Tredgold, "and there's nothing gained by delay. On Wednesday we'll take the train to Biddlecombe and have a look round. My idea is to buy a small, stout sailing-craft second-hand; ship a crew ostensibly for a pleasure trip, and sail as soon as possible."

Mr. Chalk's face brightened. "And we'll take some beads, and guns, and looking-glasses, and trade with the natives in the different islands we pass," he said, cheerfully. "We may as well see something of the world while we're about it."

Mr. Tredgold smiled indulgently and said they would see. Messrs. Stobell and Chalk, after a final glance at the map and a final perusal of the instructions at the back, took their departure.

"It's like a dream," said the latter gentleman, as they walked down the High Street.

"That Vickers girl ud like more dreams o' the same sort," said Mr. Stobell, as he thrust his hand in his empty pocket.

"It's all very well for you," continued Mr. Chalk, uneasily. "But my wife is sure to insist upon coming."

Mr. Stobell sniffed. "I've got a wife too," he remarked.

"Yes," said Mr. Chalk, in a burst of unwonted frankness, "but it ain't quite the same thing. I've got a wife and Mrs. Stobell has got a husband—that's the difference."

Mr. Stobell pondered this remark for the rest of the way home. He came to the conclusion that the events of the evening had made Mr. Chalk a little light-headed.

CHAPTER VIII

Until he stood on the platform on Wednesday morning with his brother adventurers Mr. Chalk passed the time in a state of nervous excitement, which only tended to confirm his wife in her suspicions of his behaviour. Without any preliminaries he would burst out suddenly into snatches of sea-songs, the "Bay of Biscay" being an especial favourite, until Mrs. Chalk thought fit to observe that, "if the thunder did roar like that she should not be afraid of it." Ever sensitive to a fault, Mr. Chalk fell back upon "Tom Bowling," which he thought free from openings of that sort, until Mrs. Chalk, after commenting upon the inability of the late Mr. Bowling to hear the tempest's howling, indulged in idle speculations as to what he would have thought of Mr. Chalk's. Tredgold and Stobell bought papers on the station, but Mr. Chalk was in too exalted a mood for reading. The bustle and life as the train became due were admirably attuned to his feelings, and when it drew up and they embarked, to the clatter of milk-cans and the rumbling of trolleys, he was beaming with satisfaction.

"I feel that I can smell the sea already," he remarked.

Mr. Stobell put down his paper and sniffed; then he resumed it again and, meeting Mr. Tredgold's eye over the top of it, sniffed more loudly than before.

"Have you told Edward that you are going to sea?" inquired Mr. Chalk, leaning over to Tredgold.

"Certainly not," was the reply; "I don't want anybody to know till the last possible moment. You haven't given your wife any hint as to why you are going to Biddlecombe to-day, have you?"

Mr. Chalk shook his head. "I told her that you had got business there, and that I was going with you just for the outing," he said. "What she'll say when she finds out—"

His imagination failed him and, a prey to forebodings, he tried to divert his mind by looking out of window. His countenance cleared as they neared Biddlecombe, and, the line running for some distance by the side of the river, he amused himself by gazing at various small craft left high and dry by the tide.

A short walk from the station brought them to the mouth of the river which constitutes the harbour of Biddlecombe. For a small port there was a goodly array of shipping, and Mr. Chalk's pulse beat faster as his gaze wandered impartially from a stately barque in all the pride of fresh paint to dingy, sea-worn ketches and tiny yachts.

Uncertain how to commence operations, they walked thoughtfully up and down the quay. If any of the craft were for sale there was nothing to announce the fact, and the various suggestions which Mr. Chalk threw off from time to time as to the course they should pursue were hardly noticed.

"One o'clock," said Mr. Stobell, extracting a huge silver timepiece from his pocket, after a couple of wasted hours.

"Let's have something to eat before we do any more," said Mr. Tredgold. "After that we'll ferry over and look at the other side."

They made their way to the "King of Hanover," an old inn, perched on the side of the harbour, and, mounting the stairs, entered the coffee-room, where Mr. Stobell, after hesitating for some time between the rival claims of roast beef and grilled chops, solved the difficulty by ordering both.

The only other occupant of the room, a short, wiry man, with a close-shaven, hard-bitten face, sat smoking, with a glass of whisky before him, in a bay window at the end of the room, which looked out on the harbour. There was a maritime flavour about him which at once enlisted Mr. Chalk's sympathies and made him overlook the small, steely- grey eyes and large and somewhat brutal mouth.

"Fine day, gentlemen," said the stranger, nodding affably to Mr. Chalk as he raised his glass. Mr. Chalk assented, and began a somewhat minute discussion upon the weather, which lasted until the waiter appeared with the lunch.

"Bring me another drop o' whisky, George," said the stranger, as the latter was about to leave the room, "and a little stronger, d'ye hear? A man might drink this and still be in the Band of Hope."

"We thought it wouldn't do for you to get the chuck out of it after all these years, Cap'n Brisket," said George, calmly. "It's a whisky that's kept special for teetotalers like you."

Captain Brisket gave a hoarse laugh and winked at Mr. Stobell; that gentleman, merely pausing to empty his mouth and drink half a glass of beer, winked back.

"Been here before, sir?" inquired the captain.

Mr. Stobell, who was busy again, left the reply to Mr. Chalk.

"Several times," said the latter. "I'm very fond of the sea."

Captain Brisket nodded, and, taking up his glass, moved to the end of their table, with the air of a man disposed to conversation.

"There's not much doing in Biddlecombe nowadays," he remarked, shaking his head. "Trade ain't what it used to be; ships are more than half their time looking for freights. And even when they get them they're hardly worth having."

Mr. Chalk started and, leaning over, whispered to Mr. Tredgold.

"No harm in it," said the latter. "Better leave it to me. Shipping's dull, then?" he inquired, turning to Captain Brisket.

"Dull?" was the reply. "Dull ain't no name for it."

Mr. Tredgold played with a salt-spoon and frowned thoughtfully.

"We've been looking round for a ship this morning," he said, slowly.

"As passengers?" inquired the captain, staring.

"As owners," put in Mr. Chalk.

Captain Brisket, greatly interested, drew first his glass and then his chair a yard nearer. "Do you mean that you want to buy one?" he inquired.

"Well, we might if we could get one cheap," admitted Tredgold, cautiously. "We had some sort of an idea of a cruise to the South Pacific; pleasure, with perhaps a little trading mixed up with it. I suppose some of these old schooners can be picked up for the price of an old song?"

The captain, grating his chair along the floor, came nearer still; so near that Mr. Stobell instinctively put out his right elbow.

"You've met just the right man," said Captain Brisket, with a boisterous laugh. "I know a schooner, two hundred and forty tons, that is just the identical article you're looking for, good as new and sound as a bell. Are you going to sail her yourself?"

"No," said Mr. Stobell, without looking up, "he ain't."

"Got a master?" demanded Captain Brisket, with growing excitement. "Don't tell me you've got a master."

"Why not?" growled Mr. Stobell, who, having by this time arrived at the cheese, felt that he had more leisure for conversation.

"Because," shouted the other, hitting the table a thump with his fist that upset half his whisky—"because if you haven't Bill Brisket's your man."

The three gentlemen received this startling intelligence with such a lack of enthusiasm that Captain Brisket was fain to cover what in any other man might have been regarded as confusion by ringing the bell for George and inquiring with great sternness of manner why he had not brought him a full glass.

"We can't do things in five minutes," said Mr. Tredgold, after a long and somewhat trying pause. "First of all we've got to get a ship."

"The craft you want is over the other side of the harbour waiting for you," said the captain, confidently. "We'll ferry over now if you like, or, if you prefer to go by yourselves, do; Bill Brisket is not the man to stand in anyone's way, whether he gets anything out of it or not."

"Hold hard," said Mr. Stobell, putting up his hand.

Captain Brisket regarded him with a beaming smile; Mr. Stobell's two friends waited patiently.

"What ud a schooner like that fetch?" inquired Mr. Stobell.

"It all depends," said Brisket. "Of course, if I buy—"

Mr. Stobell held up his hand again. "All depends whether you buy it for us or sell it for the man it belongs to, I s'pose?" he said, slowly.

Captain Brisket jumped up, and to Mr. Chalk's horror smote the speaker heavily on the back. Mr. Stobell, clenching a fist the size of a leg of mutton, pushed his chair back and prepared to rise.

"You're a trump," said Captain Brisket, in tones of unmistakable respect, "that's what you are. Lord, if I'd got the head for business you have I should be a man of fortune by now."

Mr. Stobell, who had half risen, sat down again, and, for the first time since his last contract but one, a smile played lightly about the corners of his mouth. He took another drink and, shaking his head slightly as he put the glass down, smiled again with the air of a man who has been reproached for making a pun.

"Let me do it for you," said Captain Brisket, impressively. "I'll tell you where to go without being seen in the matter or letting old Todd know that I'm in it. Ask him a price and bate him down; when you've got his lowest, come to me and give me one pound in every ten I save you."

Mr. Tredgold looked at his friends. "If we do that," he said, turning to the captain, "it would be to your interest to buy the ship in any case. How are we to be sure she is seaworthy?"

"Ah, there you are!" said Brisket, with an expansive smile. "You let me buy for you and promise me the master's berth, provided you are satisfied with my credentials. Common sense'll tell you I wouldn't risk my own carcass in a rotten ship."

Mr. Stobell nodded approval and, Captain Brisket with unexpected delicacy withdrawing to the window and becoming interested in the harbour, conferred for some time with his friends. The captain's offer being accepted, subject to certain conditions, they settled their bill and made their way to the ferry.

"There's the schooner," said the captain, pointing, as they neared the opposite shore; "the *Fair Emily,* and the place she is lying at is called Todd's Wharf. Ask for Mr. Todd, or, better still, walk straight on to the wharf and have a look at her. The old man'll see you fast enough."

He sprang nimbly ashore as the boat's head touched the stairs, and after extending a hand to Mr. Chalk, which was coldly ignored, led the way up the steps to the quay.

"There's the wharf just along there," he said, pointing up the road. "I'll wait for you at the Jack Ashore here. Don't offer him too much to begin with."

"I thought of offering a hundred pounds," said Mr. Tredgold. "If the ship's sound we can't be very much out over that sum."

Captain Brisket stared at him. "No; don't do that," he said, recovering, and speaking with great gravity. "Offer him seventy. Good luck."

He watched them up the road and then, with a mysterious grin, turned into the Jack Ashore, and taking a seat in the bar waited patiently for their return.

Half an hour passed. The captain had smoked one pipe and was half through another. He glanced at the clock over the bar and fidgeted as an unpleasant idea that the bargain, despite Mr. Tredgold's ideas as to the value of schooners, might have been completed without his assistance occurred to him. He took a sip from his glass, and then his face softened as the faint sounds of a distant uproar broke upon his ear.

"What's that?" said a customer.

The landlord, who was glancing at the paper, put it down and listened. "Sounds like old Todd at it again," he said, coming round to the front of the bar.

The noise came closer. "It is old Todd," said another customer, and hastily finishing his beer moved with the others to the door. Captain Brisket, with a fine air of indifference, lounged after them, and peering over their shoulders obtained a good view of the approaching disturbance.

His three patrons, with a hopeless attempt to appear unconcerned, were coming down the road, while close behind a respectable-looking old gentleman with a long, white beard and a voice like a foghorn almost danced with excitement. They quickened their pace as they neared the inn, and Mr. Chalk, throwing appearances to the winds, almost dived through the group at the door. He was at once followed by Mr. Tredgold, but Mr. Stobell, black with wrath, paused in the doorway.

"FETCH'EM OUT," vociferated the old gentleman as the landlord barred the doorway with his arms. "Fetch that red-whiskered one out and I'll eat him."

"What's the matter, Mr. Todd?" inquired the landlord, with a glance at his friends. "What's he done?"

"*Done?*" repeated the excitable Mr. Todd.

"Done? They come walking on to my wharf as if the place—FETCH HIM OUT," he bawled, breaking off suddenly. "Fetch him out and I'll skin him alive."

Captain Brisket took Mr. Stobell by the cuff and after a slight altercation drew him inside.

"Tell that red-whiskered man to come outside," bawled Mr. Todd. "What's he afraid of?"

"What have you been doing to him?" inquired Captain Brisket, turning to the pallid Mr. Chalk.

"Nothing," was the reply.

"Is he coming out?" demanded the terrible voice, "or have I got to wait here all night? Why don't he come outside, and I'll break every bone in his body."

Mr. Stobell scratched his head in gloomy perplexity; then, as his gaze fell upon the smiling countenances of Mr. Todd's fellow-townsmen, his face cleared.

"He's an old man," he said, slowly, "but if any of you would like to step outside with me for five minutes, you've only got to say the word, you know."

Nobody manifesting any signs of accepting this offer, he turned away and took a seat by the side of the indignant Tredgold. Mr. Todd, after a final outburst, began to feel exhausted, and forsaking his prey with much reluctance allowed himself to be led away. Snatches of a strong and copious benediction, only partly mellowed by distance, fell upon the ears of the listeners.

"Did you offer him the seventy?" inquired Captain Brisket, turning to Mr. Tredgold.

"I did," said Mr. Chalk, plaintively.

"Ah," said the captain, regarding him thoughtfully; "perhaps you ought to ha' made it eighty. He's asking eight hundred for it, I understand."

Mr. Tredgold turned sharply. "Eight hundred?" he gasped.

The captain nodded. "And I'm not saying it's not worth it," he said, "but I might be able to get it for you for six. You'd better leave it to me now."

Mr. Tredgold at first said he would have nothing more to do with it, but under the softening influence of a pipe and a glass was induced to reconsider his decision. Captain Brisket, waving farewells from the quay as they embarked on the ferryboat later on in the afternoon, bore in his pocket the cards of all three gentlemen, together with a commission entrusting him with the preliminary negotiations for the purchase of the Fair Emily.

CHAPTER IX

The church bells were ringing for morning service as Mr. Vickers, who had been for a stroll with Mr. William Russell and a couple of ferrets, returned home to breakfast. Contrary to custom, the small front room and the kitchen were both empty, and breakfast, with the exception of a cold herring and the bitter remains of a pot of tea, had been cleared away.

"I've known men afore now," murmured Mr. Vickers, eyeing the herring disdainfully, "as would take it by the tail and smack'em acrost the face with it."

He cut himself a slice of bread, and, pouring out a cup of cold tea, began his meal, ever and anon stopping to listen, with a puzzled face, to a continuous squeaking overhead. It sounded like several pairs of new boots all squeaking at once, but Mr. Vickers, who was a reasonable man and past the age of self-deception, sought for a more probable cause.

A particularly aggressive squeak detached itself from the others and sounded on the stairs. The resemblance to the noise made by new boots was stronger than ever. It was new boots. The door opened, and Mr. Vickers, with a slice of bread arrested half-way to his mouth, sat gazing in astonishment at Charles Vickers, clad for the first time in his life in new raiment from top to toe. Ere he could voice inquiries, an avalanche of squeaks descended the stairs, and the rest of the children, all smartly clad, with Selina bringing up the rear, burst into the room.

"What is it?" demanded Mr. Vickers, in a voice husky with astonishment; "a bean-feast?"

Miss Vickers, who was doing up a glove which possessed more buttons than his own waistcoat, looked up and eyed him calmly. "New clothes—and not before they wanted'em," she replied, tartly.

"New clothes?" repeated her father, in a scandalized voice. "Where'd they get'em?"

"Shop," said his daughter, briefly.

Mr. Vickers rose and, approaching his offspring, inspected them with the same interest that he would have bestowed upon a wax-works. A certain stiffness of pose combined with the glassy stare which met his gaze helped to favour the illusion.

"For once in their lives they're respectable," said Selina, regarding them with moist eyes. "Soap and water they've always had, bless'em, but you've never seen'em dressed like this before."

Before Mr. Vickers could frame a reply a squeaking which put all the others in the shade sounded from above. It crossed the floor on hurried excursions to different parts of the room, and then, hesitating for a moment at the head of the stairs, came slowly and ponderously down until Mrs. Vickers, looking somewhat nervous, stood revealed before her expectant husband. In scornful surprise he gazed at a blue cloth dress, a black velvet cape trimmed with bugles, and a bonnet so aggressively new that it had not yet accommodated itself to Mrs. Vickers's style of hair-dressing.

"Go on!" he breathed. "Go on! Don't mind me. What, you—you—you're not going to church?"

Mrs. Vickers glanced at the books in her hand—also new—and trembled.

"And why not?" demanded Selina. "Why shouldn't we?"

Mr. Vickers took another amazed glance round and his brow darkened.

"Where did you get the money?" he inquired.

"Saved it," said his daughter, reddening despite herself.

"Saved it?" repeated the justly-astonished Mr. Vickers. "Saved it? Ah! out of my money; out of the money I toil and moil for—out of the money that ought to be spent on food. No wonder you're always complaining that it ain't enough. I won't 'ave it, d'ye hear? I'll have my rights; I'll——"

"Don't make so much noise," said his daughter, who was stooping down to ease one of Mrs. Vickers's boots. "You would have fours, mother, and I told you what it would be."

"He said that I ought to wear threes by rights," said Mrs. Vickers; "I used to."

"And I s'pose," said Mr. Vickers, who had been listening to these remarks with considerable impatience—"I s'pose there's a bran' new suit o' clothes, and a pair o' boots, and 'arf-a-dozen shirts, and a new hat hid upstairs for me?"

"Yes, they're hid all right," retorted the dutiful Miss Vickers. "You go upstairs and amuse yourself looking for'em. Go and have a game of 'hot boiled beans' all by yourself."

"Why, you must have been stinting me for years," continued Mr. Vickers, examining the various costumes in detail. "This is what comes o' keeping quiet and trusting you—not but what I've 'ad my suspicions. My own kids taking the bread out o' my mouth and buying boots with it; my own wife going about in a bonnet that's took me weeks and weeks to earn."

His words fell on deaf ears. No adjutant getting his regiment ready for a march-past could have taken more trouble than Miss Vickers was taking at this moment over her small company. Caps were set straight and sleeves pulled down. Her face shone with pride and her eyes glistened as the small fry, discoursing in excited whispers, filed stiffly out.

A sudden cessation of gossip in neighbouring doorways testified to the impression made by their appearance. Past little startled groups the procession picked its way in squeaking pride, with Mrs. Vickers and Selina bringing up the rear. The children went by with little set, important faces; but Miss Vickers's little bows and pleased smiles of recognition to acquaintances were so lady-like that several untidy matrons retired inside their houses to wrestle grimly with feelings too strong for outside display.

"Pack o' prancing peacocks," said the unnatural Mr. Vickers, as the procession wound round the corner.

He stood looking vacantly up the street until the gathering excitement of his neighbours aroused new feelings. Vanity stirred within him, and leaning casually against the door-post he yawned and looked at the chimney-pots opposite. A neighbour in a pair of corduroy trousers, supported by one brace worn diagonally, shambled across the road.

"What's up?" he inquired, with a jerk of the thumb in the direction of Mr. Vickers's vanished family.

"Up?" repeated Mr. Vickers, with an air of languid surprise.

"Somebody died and left you a fortin?" inquired the other.

"Not as I knows of," replied Mr. Vickers, staring. "Why?"

"Why?" exclaimed the other. "Why, new clothes all over. I never see such a turn-out."

Mr. Vickers regarded him with an air of lofty disdain. "Kids must 'ave new clothes sometimes, I s'pose?" he said, slowly. "You wouldn't 'ave'em going about of a Sunday in a ragged shirt and a pair of trowsis, would you?"

The shaft passed harmlessly. "Why not?" said the other. "They gin'rally do."

Mr. Vickers's denial died away on his lips. In twos and threes his neighbours had drawn gradually near and now stood by listening expectantly. The idea of a fortune was common to all of them, and they were anxious for particulars.

"Some people have all the luck," said a stout matron. "I've 'ad thirteen and buried seven, and never 'ad so much as a chiney tea-pot left me. One thing is, I never could make up to people for the sake of what I could get out of them. I couldn't not if I tried. I must speak my mind free and independent."

"Ah! that's how you get yourself disliked," said another lady, shaking her head sympathetically.

"Disliked?" said the stout matron, turning on her fiercely. "What d'ye mean? You don't know what you're talking about. Who's getting themselves disliked?"

"A lot o' good a chiney tea-pot would be to you," said the other, with a ready change of front, "or any other kind o' tea-pot."

Surprise and indignation deprived the stout matron of utterance.

"Or a milk-jug either," pursued her opponent, following up her advantage. "Or a coffee-pot, or—"

The stout matron advanced upon her, and her mien was so terrible that the other, retreating to her house, slammed the door behind her and continued the discussion from a first-floor window. Mint Street, with the conviction that Mr. Vickers's tidings could wait, swarmed across the road to listen.

Mr. Vickers himself listened for a little while to such fragments as came his way, and then, going indoors, sat down amid the remains of his breakfast to endeavour to solve the mystery of the new clothes.

He took a short clay pipe from his pocket, and, igniting a little piece of tobacco which remained in the bowl, endeavoured to form an estimate of the cost of each person's wardrobe. The sum soon becoming too large to work in his head, he had recourse to pencil and paper, and after five minutes' hard labour sat gazing at a total which made his brain reel. The fact that immediately afterwards he was unable to find even a few grains of tobacco at the bottom of his box furnished a contrast which almost made him maudlin.

He sat sucking at his cold pipe and indulging in hopeless conjectures as to the source of so much wealth, and, with a sudden quickening of the pulse, wondered whether it had all been spent. His mind wandered from Selina to Mr. Joseph Tasker, and almost imperceptibly the absurdities of which young men in love could be capable occurred to him. He remembered the extravagances of his own youth, and bethinking himself of the sums he had squandered on the future Mrs. Vickers—sums which increased with the compound interest of repetition—came to the conclusion that Mr. Tasker had been more foolish still.

It seemed the only possible explanation. His eye brightened, and, knocking the ashes out of his pipe, he crossed to the tap and washed his face.

"If he can't lend a trifle to the man what's going to be his father-in-law," he said, cheerfully, as he polished his face on a roller-towel, "I shall tell 'im he can't have Selina, that's all. I'll go and see 'im afore she gets any more out of him."

He walked blithely up the road, and, after shaking off one or two inquirers whose curiosity was almost proof against insult, made his way to Dialstone Lane. In an unobtrusive fashion he glided round to the back, and, opening the kitchen door, bestowed a beaming smile upon the startled Joseph.

"Busy, my lad?" he inquired.

"What d'ye want?" asked Mr. Tasker, whose face was flushed with cooking.

Mr. Vickers opened the door a little wider, and, stepping inside, closed it softly behind him and dropped into a chair.

"Don't be alarmed, my lad," he said, benevolently. "Selina's all right."

"What d'ye want?" repeated Mr. Tasker. "Who told you to come round here?"

Mr. Vickers looked at him in reproachful surprise.

"I suppose a father can come round to see his future son-in-law?" he said, with some dignity. "I don't want to do no interrupting of your work, Joseph, but I couldn't 'elp just stepping round to tell you how nice they all looked. Where you got the money from I can't think."

"Have you gone dotty, or what?" demanded Mr. Tasker, who was busy wiping out a saucepan. "Who looked nice?"

Mr. Vickers shook his head at him and smiled waggishly.

"Ah! who?" he said, with much enjoyment. "I tell you it did my father's 'art good to see 'em all dressed up like that; and when I thought of its all being owing to you, sit down at home in comfort with a pipe instead of coming to thank you for it I could not. Not if you was to have paid me I couldn't."

"Look 'ere," said Mr. Tasker, putting the saucepan down with a bang, "if you can't talk plain, common English you'd better get out. I don't want you 'ere at all as a matter o' fact, but to have you sitting there shaking your silly 'ead and talking a pack o' nonsense is more than I can stand."

Mr. Vickers gazed at him in perplexity. "Do you mean to tell me you haven't been giving my Selina money to buy new clothes for the young'uns?" he demanded, sharply. "Do you mean to tell me that Selina didn't get money out of you to buy herself and 'er mother and all of 'em— except me—a new rig-out from top to toe?"

"D'ye think I've gone mad, or what?" inquired the amazed Mr. Tasker. "What d'ye think I should want to buy clothes for your young'uns for? That's your duty. And Selina, too; I haven't given 'er anything except a ring, and she lent me the money for that. D'ye think I'm made o' money?"

"All right, Joseph," said Mr. Vickers, secretly incensed at this unforeseen display of caution on Mr. Tasker's part. "I s'pose the fairies come and put'em on while they was asleep. But it's dry work walking; 'ave you got such a thing as a glass o' water you could give me?"

The other took a glass from the dresser and, ignoring the eye of his prospective father-in-law, which was glued to a comfortable-looking barrel in the corner, filled it to the brim with fair water and handed it to him. Mr. Vickers, giving him a surly nod, took a couple of dainty sips and placed it on the table.

"It's very nice water," he said, sarcastically.

"Is it?" said Mr. Tasker. "We don't drink it ourselves, except in tea or coffee; the cap'n says it ain't safe."

Mr. Vickers brought his eye from the barrel and glared at him.

"I s'pose, Joseph," he said, after a long pause, during which Mr. Tasker was busy making up the fire—"I s'pose Selina didn't tell you you wasn't to tell me about the money?"

"I don't know what you're driving at," said the other, confronting him angrily. "I haven't got no money."

Mr. Vickers coughed. "Don't say that, Joseph," he urged, softly; "don't say that, my lad. As a matter o' fact, I come round to you, interrupting of you in your work, and I'm sorry for it—knowing how fond of it you are—to see whether I couldn't borrow a trifle for a day or two."

"Ho, did you?" commented Mr. Tasker, who had opened the oven door and was using his hand as a thermometer.

His visitor hesitated. It was no use asking for too much; on the other hand, to ask for less than he could get would be unpardonable folly.

"If I could lay my hand on a couple o' quid," he said, in a mysterious whisper, "I could make it five in a week."

"Well, why don't you?" inquired Mr. Tasker, who was tenderly sucking the bulb of the thermometer after contact with the side of the oven.

"It's the two quid that's the trouble, Joseph," replied Mr. Vickers, keeping his temper with difficulty. "A little thing like that wouldn't be much trouble to you, I know, but to a pore man with a large family like me it's a'most impossible."

Mr. Tasker went outside to the larder, and returning with a small joint knelt down and thrust it carefully into the oven.

"A'most impossible," repeated Mr. Vickers, with a sigh.

"What is?" inquired the other, who had not been listening.

The half-choking Mr. Vickers explained.

"Yes, o' course it is," assented Mr. Tasker.

"People what's got money," said the offended Mr. Vickers, regarding him fiercely, "stick to it like leeches. Now, suppose I was a young man keeping company with a gal and her father wanted to borrow a couple o' quid—a paltry couple o' thick'uns—what d'ye think I should do?"

"If you was a young man—keeping company with a gal—and 'er father wanted—to borrow a couple of quid off o' you—what would you do?" repeated Mr. Tasker, mechanically, as he bustled to and fro.

Mr. Vickers nodded and smiled. "What should I do?" he inquired again, hopefully.

"I don't know, I'm sure," said the other, opening the oven door and peering in. "How should I?"

At the imminent risk of something inside giving way under the strain, Mr. Vickers restrained himself. He breathed hard, and glancing out of window sought to regain his equilibrium by becoming interested in a blackbird outside.

"What I mean to say is," he said at length, in a trembling voice—"what I mean to say is, without no round-aboutedness, will you lend a 'ard-working man, what's going to be your future father-in-law, a couple o' pounds?"

Mr. Tasker laughed. It was not a loud laugh, nor yet a musical one. It was merely a laugh designed to convey to the incensed Mr. Vickers a strong sense of the absurdity of his request.

"I asked you a question," said the latter gentleman, glaring at him.

"I haven't got a couple o' pounds," replied Mr. Tasker; "and if I 'ad, there's nine hundred and ninety-nine things I would sooner do with it than lend it to you."

Mr. Vickers rose and stood regarding the ignoble creature with profound contempt. His features worked and a host of adjectives crowded to his lips.

"Is that your last word, Joseph?" he inquired, with solemn dignity.

"I'll say it all over again if you like," said the obliging Mr. Tasker. "If you want money, go and earn it, same as I have to; don't come round 'ere cadging on me, because it's no good."

Mr. Vickers laughed; a dry, contemptuous laugh, terrible to hear.

"And that's the man that's going to marry my daughter," he said, slowly; "that's the man that's going to marry into my family. Don't you expect me to take you up and point you out as my son-in-law, cos I won't do it. If there's anything I can't abide it's stinginess. And there's my gal —my pore gal don't know your real character. Wait till I've told 'er about this morning and opened 'er eyes! Wait till—"

He stopped abruptly as the door leading to the front room opened and revealed the inquiring face of Captain Bowers.

"What's all this noise about, Joseph?" demanded the captain, harshly.

Mr. Tasker attempted to explain, but his explanation involving a character for Mr. Vickers which that gentleman declined to accept on any terms, he broke in and began to give his own version of the affair. Much to Joseph's surprise the captain listened patiently.

"Did you buy all those things, Joseph?" he inquired, carelessly, as Mr. Vickers paused for breath.

"Cert'nly not, sir," replied Mr. Tasker. "Where should I get the money from?"

The captain eyed him without replying, and a sudden suspicion occurred to him. The strange disappearance of the map, followed by the sudden cessation of Mr. Chalk's visits, began to link themselves to this tale of unexpected wealth. He bestowed another searching glance upon the agitated Mr. Tasker.

"You haven't sold anything lately, have you?" he inquired, with startling gruffness.

"I haven't 'ad nothing to sell, sir," replied the other, in astonishment. "And I dare say Mr. Vickers here saw a new pair o' boots on one o' the young'uns and dreamt all the rest."

Mr. Vickers intervened with passion.

"That'll do," said the captain, sharply. "How dare you make that noise in my house? I think that the tale about the clothes is all right," he added, turning to Joseph. "I saw them go into church looking very smart. And you know nothing about it?"

Mr. Tasker's astonishment was too genuine to be mistaken, and the captain, watching him closely, transferred his suspicions to a more deserving object. Mr. Vickers caught his eye and essayed a smile.

"Dry work talking, sir," he said, gently.

Captain Bowers eyed him steadily. "Have we got any beer, Joseph?" he inquired.

"Plenty in the cask, sir," said Mr. Tasker, reluctantly.

"Well, keep your eye on it," said the captain. "Good morning, Mr. Vickers."

But disappointment and indignation got the better of Mr. Vickers's politeness.

CHAPTER X

"Penny for your thoughts, uncle," said Miss Drewitt, as they sat at dinner an hour or two after the departure of Mr. Vickers.

"*H'm?*" said the captain, with a guilty start. "You've been scowling and smiling by turns for the last five minutes," said his niece.

"I was thinking about that man that was here this morning," said the captain, slowly; "trying to figure it out. If I thought that that girl Selina—"

He took a draught of ale and shook his head solemnly.

"You know my ideas about that," said Prudence.

"Your poor mother was obstinate," commented the captain, regarding her tolerantly. "Once she got an idea into her head it stuck there, and nothing made her more angry than proving to her that she was wrong. Trying to prove to her, I should have said."

Miss Drewitt smiled amiably. "Well, you've earned half the sum," she said. "Now, what were you smiling about?"

"Didn't know I was smiling," declared the captain.

With marvellous tact he turned the conversation to lighthouses, a subject upon which he discoursed with considerable fluency until the meal was finished. Miss Drewitt, who had a long memory and at least her fair share of curiosity, returned to the charge as he smoked half a pipe preparatory to accompanying her for a walk.

"You're looking very cheerful," she remarked.

The captain's face fell several points. "Am I?" he said, ruefully. "I didn't mean to."

"Why not?" inquired his niece.

"I mean I didn't know I was," he replied, "more than usual, I mean. I always do look fairly cheerful—at least, I hope I do. There's nothing to make me look the opposite."

Miss Drewitt eyed him carefully and then passed upstairs to put on her hat. Relieved of her presence the captain walked to the small glass over the mantelpiece and, regarding his tell-tale features with gloomy dissatisfaction, acquired, after one or two attempts, an expression which he flattered himself defied analysis.

He tapped the barometer which hung by the door as they went out, and, checking a remark which rose to his lips, stole a satisfied glance at the face by his side.

"Clark's farm by the footpaths would be a nice walk," said Miss Drewitt, as they reached the end of the lane.

The captain started. "I was thinking of Dutton Priors," he said, slowly. "We could go there by Hanger's Lane and home by the road."

"The footpaths would be nice to-day," urged his niece.

"You try my way," said the captain, jovially.

"Have you got any particular reason for wanting to go to Dutton Priors this afternoon?" inquired the girl.

"Reason?" said the captain. "Good gracious, no. What reason should I have? My leg is a trifle stiff to-day for stiles, but still—"

Miss Drewitt gave way at once, and, taking his arm, begged him to lean on her, questioning him anxiously as to his fitness for a walk in any direction.

"Walking'll do it good," was the reply, as they proceeded slowly down the High Street.

He took his watch from his pocket, and, after comparing it with the town clock, peered furtively right and left, gradually slackening his pace until Miss Drewitt's fears for his leg became almost contagious. At the old stone bridge, spanning the river at the bottom of the High Street, he paused, and, resting his arms on the parapet, became intent on a derelict punt. On the subject of sitting in a craft of that description in mid-stream catching fish he discoursed at such length that the girl eyed him in amazement.

"Shall we go on?" she said, at length.

The captain turned and, merely pausing to point out the difference between the lines of a punt and a dinghy, with a digression to sampans which included a criticism of the Chinese as boat-builders, prepared to depart. He cast a swift glance up the road as he did so, and Miss Drewitt's cheek flamed with sudden wrath as she saw Mr. Edward Tredgold hastening towards them. In a somewhat pointed manner she called her uncle's attention to the fact.

"Lor' bless my soul," said that startled mariner, "so it is. Well! well!"

If Mr. Tredgold had been advancing on his head he could not have exhibited more surprise.

"I'm afraid I'm late," said Tredgold, as he came up and shook hands. "I hope you haven't been waiting long."

The hapless captain coughed loud and long. He emerged from a large red pocket-handkerchief to find the eye of Miss Drewitt seeking his.

"That's all right, my lad," he said, huskily. "I'd forgotten about our arrangement. Did I say this Sunday or next?"

"This," said Mr. Tredgold, bluntly.

The captain coughed again, and with some pathos referred to the tricks which old age plays with memory. As they walked on he regaled them with selected instances.

"Don't forget your leg, uncle," said Miss Drewitt, softly.

Captain Bowers gazed at her suspiciously.

"Don't forget that it's stiff and put too much strain on it," explained his niece.

The captain eyed her uneasily, but she was talking and laughing with Edward Tredgold in a most reassuring fashion. A choice portion of his programme, which, owing to the events of the afternoon, he had almost resolved to omit, clamoured for production. He stole another glance at his niece and resolved to risk it.

"Hah!" he said, suddenly, stopping short and feeling in his pockets. "There's my memory again. Well, of all the—"

"What's the matter, uncle?" inquired Miss Drewitt.

"I've left my pipe at home," said the captain, in a desperate voice.

"I've got some cigars," suggested Tredgold.

The captain shook his head. "No, I must have my pipe," he said, decidedly. "If you two will walk on slowly, I'll soon catch you up."

"You're not going all the way back for it?" exclaimed Miss Drewitt.

"Let me go," said Tredgold.

The captain favoured him with an inscrutable glance. "I'll go," he said, firmly. "I'm not quite sure where I left it. You go by Hanger's Lane; I'll soon catch you up."

He set off at a pace which rendered protest unavailing. Mr. Tredgold turned, and, making a mental note of the fact that Miss Drewitt had suddenly added inches to her stature, walked on by her side.

"Captain Bowers is very fond of his pipe," he said, after they had walked a little way in silence.

Miss Drewitt assented. "Nasty things," she said, calmly.

"So they are," said Mr. Tredgold.

"But you smoke," said the girl.

Mr. Tredgold sighed. "I have often thought of giving it up," he said, softly, "and then I was afraid that it would look rather presumptuous."

"Presumptuous?" repeated Miss Drewitt.

"So many better and wiser men than myself smoke," exclaimed Mr. Tredgold, "including even bishops. If it is good enough for them, it ought to be good enough for me; that's the way I look at it. Who am I that I should be too proud to smoke? Who am I that I should try and set my poor ideas above those of my superiors? Do you see my point of view?"

Miss Drewitt made no reply.

"Of course, it is a thing that grows on one," continued Mr. Tredgold, with the air of making a concession. "It is the first smoke that does the mischief; it is a fatal precedent. Unless, perhaps—How pretty that field is over there."

Miss Drewitt looked in the direction indicated. "Very nice," she said, briefly. "But what were you going to say?"

Mr. Tredgold made an elaborate attempt to appear confused. "I was going to say," he murmured, gently, "unless, perhaps, one begins on coarse-cut Cavendish rolled in a piece of the margin of the Sunday newspaper."

Miss Drewitt suppressed an exclamation. "I wanted to see where the fascination was," she indignantly.

"And did you?" inquired Mr. Tredgold, smoothly.

The girl turned her head and looked at him. "I have no doubt my uncle gave you full particulars," she said, bitterly. "It seems to me that men can gossip as much as women."

"I tried to stop him," said the virtuous Mr. Tredgold.

"You need not have troubled," said Miss Drewitt, loftily. "It is not a matter of any consequence. I am surprised that my uncle should have thought it worth mentioning."

She walked on slowly with head erect, pausing occasionally to look round for the captain. Edward Tredgold looked too, and a feeling of annoyance at the childish stratagems of his well-meaning friend began to possess him.

"We had better hurry a little, I think," he said, glancing at the sky. "The sooner we get to Dutton Priors the better."

"Why?" inquired his companion.

"Rain," said the other, briefly.

"It won't rain before evening," said Miss Drewitt, confidently; "uncle said so."

"Perhaps we had better walk faster, though," urged Mr. Tredgold.

Miss Drewitt slackened her pace deliberately. "There is no fear of its raining," she declared. "And uncle will not catch us up if we walk fast."

A sudden glimpse into the immediate future was vouchsafed to Mr. Tredgold; for a fraction of a second the veil was lifted. "Don't blame me if you get wet through," he said, with some anxiety.

They walked on at a pace which gave the captain every opportunity of overtaking them. The feat would not have been beyond the powers of an athletic tortoise, but the most careful scrutiny failed to reveal any signs of him.

"I'm afraid that he is not well," said Miss Drewitt, after a long, searching glance along the way they had come. "Perhaps we had better go back. It does begin to look rather dark."

"Just as you please," said Edward Tredgold, with unwonted caution; "but the nearest shelter is Dutton Priors."

He pointed to a lurid, ragged cloud right ahead of them. As if in response, a low, growling rumble sounded overhead.

"Was—was that thunder?" said Miss Drewitt, drawing a little nearer to him.

"Sounded something like it," was the reply.

A flash of lightning and a crashing peal that rent the skies put the matter beyond a doubt. Miss Drewitt, turning very pale, began to walk at a rapid pace in the direction of the village.

The other looked round in search of some nearer shelter. Already the pattering of heavy drops sounded in the lane, and before they had gone a dozen paces the rain came down in torrents. Two or three fields away a small shed offered the only shelter. Mr. Tredgold, taking his companion by the arm, started to run towards it.

Before they had gone a hundred yards they were wet through, but Miss Drewitt, holding her skirts in one hand and shivering at every flash, ran until they brought up at a tall gate, ornamented with barbed wire, behind which stood the shed.

The gate was locked, and the wire had been put on by a farmer who combined with great ingenuity a fervent hatred of his fellow-men. To Miss Drewitt it seemed insurmountable, but, aided by Mr. Tredgold and a peal of thunder which came to his assistance at a critical moment, she managed to clamber over and reach the shed. Mr. Tredgold followed at his leisure with a strip of braid torn from the bottom of her dress.

The roof leaked in twenty places and the floor was a puddle, but it had certain redeeming features in Mr. Tredgold's eyes of which the girl knew nothing. He stood at the doorway watching the rain.

"Come inside," said Miss Drewitt, in a trembling voice. "You might be struck."

Mr. Tredgold experienced a sudden sense of solemn pleasure in this unexpected concern for his safety. He turned and eyed her.

"I'm not afraid," he said, with great gentleness.

"No, but I am," said Miss Drewitt, petulantly, "and I can never get over that gate alone."

Mr. Tredgold came inside, and for some time neither of them spoke. The rattle of rain on the roof became less deafening and began to drip through instead of forming little jets. A patch of blue sky showed.

"It isn't much," said Tredgold, going to the door again.

Miss Drewitt, checking a sharp retort, returned to the door and looked out. The patch of blue increased in size; the rain ceased and the sun came out; birds exchanged congratulations from every tree. The girl, gathering up her wet skirts, walked to the gate, leaving her companion to follow.

Approached calmly and under a fair sky the climb was much easier.

"I believe that I could have got over by myself after all," said Miss Drewitt, as she stood on the other side. "I suppose that you were in too much of a hurry the last time. My dress is ruined."

She spoke calmly, but her face was clouded. From her manner during the rapid walk home Mr. Tredgold was enabled to see clearly that she was holding him responsible for the captain's awkward behaviour; the rain; her spoiled clothes; and a severe cold in the immediate future. He glanced at her ruined hat and the wet, straight locks of hair hanging about her face, and held his peace.

Never before on a Sunday afternoon had Miss Drewitt known the streets of Binchester to be so full of people. She hurried on with bent head, looking straight before her, trying to imagine what she looked like. There was no sign of the captain, but as they turned into Dialstone Lane they both saw a huge, shaggy, grey head protruding from the small window of his bedroom. It disappeared with a suddenness almost startling.

"Thank you," said Miss Drewitt, holding out her hand as she reached the door. "Good-bye."

Mr. Tredgold said "Good-bye," and with a furtive glance at the window above departed. Miss Drewitt, opening the door, looked round an empty room. Then the kitchen door opened and the face of Mr. Tasker, full of concern, appeared.

"Did you get wet, miss?" he inquired.

Miss Drewitt ignored the question. "Where is Captain Bowers?" she asked, in a clear, penetrating voice.

The face of Mr. Tasker fell. "He's gone to bed with a headache, miss," he replied.

"Headache?" repeated the astonished Miss Drewitt. "When did he go?"

"About 'arf an hour ago," said Mr. Tasker; "just after the storm. I suppose that's what caused it, though it seems funny, considering what a lot he must ha' seen at sea. He said he'd go straight to bed and try and sleep it off. And I was to ask you to please not to make a noise."

Miss Drewitt swept past him and mounted the stairs. At the captain's door she paused, but the loud snoring of a determined man made her resolve to postpone her demands for an explanation to a more fitting opportunity. Tired, wet, and angry she gained her own room, and threw herself thoughtlessly into that famous old Chippendale chair which, in accordance with Mr. Tredgold's instructions, had been placed against the wall.

The captain started in his sleep.

CHAPTER XI

Mr. Chalk's anxiety during the negotiations for the purchase of the *Fair Emily* kept him oscillating between Tredgold and Stobell until those gentlemen fled at his approach and instructed their retainers to make untruthful statements as to their whereabouts. Daily letters from Captain Brisket stated that he was still haggling with Mr. Todd over the price, and Mr. Chalk quailed as he tried to picture the scene with that doughty champion.

Three times at the earnest instigation of his friends, who pointed out the necessity of keeping up appearances, had he set out to pay a visit to Dialstone Lane, and three times had he turned back half-way as he realized the difficult nature of his task. As well ask a poacher to call on a gamekeeper the morning after a raid.

Captain Bowers, anxious to see him and sound him with a few carefully- prepared questions, noted his continued absence with regret. Despairing at last of a visit from Mr. Chalk, he resolved to pay one himself.

Mr. Chalk, who was listening to his wife, rose hastily at his entrance, and in great confusion invited him to a chair which was already occupied by Mrs. Chalk's work-basket. The captain took another and, after listening to an incoherent statement about the weather, shook his head reproachfully at Mr. Chalk.

"I thought something must have happened to you," he said. "Why, it must be weeks since I've seen you."

"Weeks?" said Mrs. Chalk, suddenly alert.

"Why, he went out the day before yesterday to call on you."

"Yes," said Mr. Chalk, with an effort, "so I did, but half-way to yours I got a nail in my shoe and had to come home."

"Home!" exclaimed his wife. "Why, you were gone two hours and thirty-five minutes."

"It was very painful," said Mr. Chalk, as the captain stared in open-eyed astonishment at this exact time-keeping. "One time I thought that I should hardly have got back."

"But you didn't say anything about it," persisted his wife.

"I didn't want to alarm you, my dear," said Mr. Chalk.

Mrs. Chalk looked at him, but, except for a long, shivering sigh which the visitor took for sympathy, made no comment.

"I often think that I must have missed a great deal by keeping single," said the latter. "It must be very pleasant when you're away to know that there is somebody at home counting the minutes until your return."

Mr. Chalk permitted himself one brief wondering glance in the speaker's direction, and then gazed out of window.

"There's no companion like a wife," continued the captain. "Nobody else can quite share your joys and sorrows as she can. I've often thought how pleasant it must be to come home from a journey and tell your wife all about it: where you've been, what you've done, and what you're going to do."

Mr. Chalk stole another look at him; Mrs. Chalk, somewhat suspicious, followed his example.

"It's a pity you never married, Captain Bowers," she said, at length; "most men seem to do all they can to keep things from their wives. But one of these days——"

She finished the sentence by an expressive glance at her husband. Captain Bowers, suddenly enlightened, hastened to change the subject.

"I haven't seen Tredgold or Stobell either," he said, gazing fixedly at Mr. Chalk.

"They—they were talking about you only the other day," said that gentleman, nervously. "Is Miss Drewitt well?"

"Quite well," said the captain, briefly. "I was beginning to think you had all left Binchester," he continued; "gone for a sea voyage or something."

Mr. Chalk laughed uneasily. "I thought that Joseph wasn't looking very well the last time I saw you," he said, with an imploring glance at the captain to remind him of the presence of Mrs. Chalk.

"Joseph's all right," replied the other, "so is the parrot."

Mr. Chalk started and said that he was glad to hear it, and sat trying to think of a safe subject for conversation.

"Joseph's a nice parrot," he said at last. "The parrot's a nice lad, I mean."

"Thomas!" said Mrs. Chalk.

"Joseph-is-a-nice-lad," said Mr. Chalk, recovering himself. "I have often thought——"

The sentence was never completed, being interrupted by a thundering rat-tat-tat at the front door, followed by a pealing at the bell, which indicated that the visitor was manfully following the printed injunction to "Ring also." The door was opened and a man's voice was heard in the hall-a loud, confident voice, at the sound of which Mr. Chalk, with one horrified glance in the direction of Captain Bowers, sank back in his chair and held his breath.

"Captain Brisket," said the maid, opening the door.

The captain came in with a light, bustling step, and, having shaken Mr. Chalk's hand with great fervour and acknowledged the presence of Captain Bowers and Mrs. Chalk by two spasmodic jerks of the head, sat bolt-upright on the edge of a chair and beamed brightly upon the horrified Chalk.

"I've got news," he said, hoarsely.

"News?" said the unfortunate Mr. Chalk, faintly.

"Ah!" said Brisket, nodding. "News! I've got her at last."

Mrs. Chalk started.

"I've got her," continued Captain Brisket, with an air of great enjoyment; "and a fine job I had of it, I can tell you. Old Todd said he couldn't bear parting with her. Once or twice I thought he meant it."

Mr. Chalk made a desperate effort to catch his eye, but in vain. It was fixed in reminiscent joy on the ceiling.

"We haggled about her for days," continued Brisket; "but at last I won. The *Fair Emily* is yours, sir."

"The fair who?" cried Mrs. Chalk, in a terrible voice. "Emily who? Emily what?"

Captain Brisket turned and regarded her in amazement.

"Emily who?" repeated Mrs. Chalk.

"Why, it's—" began Brisket.

"H'sh!" said Mr. Chalk, desperately. "It's a secret."

"It's a secret," said Captain Brisket, nodding calmly at Mrs. Chalk.

Wrath and astonishment held her for the moment breathless. Mr. Chalk, caught between his wife and Captain Bowers, fortified himself with memories of the early martyrs and gave another warning glance at Brisket. For nearly two minutes that undaunted mariner met the gaze of Mrs. Chalk without flinching.

"A—a secret?" gasped the indignant woman at last, as she turned to her husband. "You sit there and dare to tell me that?"

"It isn't my secret," said Mr. Chalk, "else I should tell you at once."

"It isn't his secret," said the complaisant Brisket.

Mrs. Chalk controlled herself by a great effort and, turning to Captain Brisket, addressed him almost calmly. "Was it Emily that came whistling over the garden-wall the other night?" she inquired.

"Whis—?" said the hapless Brisket, making a noble effort. He finished the word with a cough and gazed with protruding eyes at Mr. Chalk. The appearance of that gentleman sobered him at once.

"No," he said, slowly.

"How do you know?" inquired Mrs. Chalk.

"Because she can't whistle," replied Captain Brisket, feeling his way carefully. "And what's more, she wouldn't if she could. She's been too well brought up for that."

He gave a cunning smile at Mr. Chalk, to which that gentleman, having decided at all hazards to keep the secret from Captain Bowers, made a ghastly response, and nodded to him to proceed.

"What's she got to do with my husband?" demanded Mrs. Chalk, her voice rising despite herself.

"I'm coming to that," said Brisket, thoughtfully, as he gazed at the floor in all the agonies of composition; "Mr. Chalk is trying to get her a new place."

"New place?" said Mrs. Chalk, in a choking voice.

Captain Brisket nodded. "She ain't happy where she is," he explained, "and Mr. Chalk—out o' pure good-nature and kindness of heart—is trying to get her another, and I honour him for it."

He looked round triumphantly. Mr. Chalk, sitting open-mouthed, was regarding him with the fascinated gaze of a rabbit before a boa-constrictor. Captain Bowers was listening with an appearance of interest which in more favourable circumstances would have been very flattering.

"You said," cried Mrs. Chalk—"you said to my husband: 'The fair Emily is yours.'"

"So I did," said Brisket, anxiously—"so I did. And what I say I stick to. When I said that the—that Emily was his, I meant it. I don't say things I don't mean. That isn't Bill Brisket's way."

"And you said just now that he was getting her a place," Mrs. Chalk reminded him, grimly.

"Mr. Chalk understands what I mean," said Captain Brisket, with dignity. "When I said 'She is yours,' I meant that she is coming here."

"O-oh!" said Mrs. Chalk, breathlessly. "Oh, indeed! Oh, is she?"

"That is, if her mother'll let her come," pursued the enterprising Brisket, with a look of great artfulness at Mr. Chalk, to call his attention to the bridge he was building for him; "but the old woman's been laid up lately and talks about not being able to spare her."

Mrs. Chalk sat back helplessly in her chair and gazed from her husband to Captain Brisket, and from Captain Brisket back to her husband. Captain Brisket, red-faced and confident, sat upright on the edge of his chair as though inviting inspection; Mr. Chalk plucked nervously at his fingers. Captain Bowers suddenly broke silence.

"What's her tonnage?" he inquired abruptly, turning to Brisket.

"Two hundred and for——"

Captain Brisket stopped dead and, rubbing his nose hard with his forefinger, gazed thoughtfully at Captain Bowers.

"The *Fair Emily* is a ship," said the latter to Mrs. Chalk.

"A ship!" cried the bewildered woman. "A ship living with her invalid mother and coming to my husband to get her a place! Are you trying to screen him, too?"

"It's a ship," repeated Captain Bowers, sternly, as he sought in vain to meet the eye of Mr. Chalk; "a craft of two hundred and something tons. For some reason—best known to himself—Mr. Chalk wants the matter kept secret."

"It—it isn't my secret," faltered Mr. Chalk.

"Where's she lying?" said Captain Bowers.

Mr. Chalk hesitated. "Biddlecombe," he said, at last.

Captain Brisket laughed noisily and, smacking his leg with his open hand, smiled broadly upon the company. No response being forthcoming, he laughed again for his own edification, and sat good-humouredly waiting events.

"Is this true, Thomas?" demanded Mrs. Chalk.

"Yes, my dear," was the reply.

"Then why didn't you tell me, instead of sitting there listening to a string of falsehoods?"

"I—I wanted to give you a surprise—a pleasant little surprise," said Mr. Chalk, with a timid glance at Captain Bowers. "I have bought a share in a schooner, to go for a little cruise. Just a jaunt for pleasure."

"Tredgold, Stobell, and Chalk," said Captain Bowers, very distinctly.

"I wanted to keep it secret until it had been repainted and done up," continued Mr. Chalk, watching his wife's face anxiously, "and then Captain Brisket came in and spoilt it."

"That's me, ma'am," said the gentleman mentioned, shaking his head despairingly. "That's Bill Brisket all over. I come blundering in, and the first thing I do is to blurt out secrets; then, when I try to smooth it over—"

Mrs. Chalk paid no heed. Alluding to the schooner as "our yacht," she at once began to discuss the subject of the voyage, the dresses she would require, and the rival merits of shutting the house up or putting the servants on board wages. Under her skilful hands, aided by a few suggestions of Captain Brisket's, the *Fair Emily* was in the short space of twenty minutes transformed into one of the most luxurious yachts that ever sailed the seas. Mr. Chalk's heart failed him as he listened. His thoughts were with his partners in the enterprise, and he trembled as he thought of their comments.

"It will do Mrs. Stobell a lot of good," said his wife, suddenly.

Mr. Chalk, about to speak, checked himself and blew his nose instead. The romance of the affair was beginning to evaporate. He sat in a state of great dejection, until Captain Bowers, having learned far more than he had anticipated, shook hands with impressive gravity and took his departure.

The captain walked home deep in thought, with a prolonged stare at the windows of Tredgold's office as he passed. The present whereabouts of the map was now quite clear, and at the top of Dialstone Lane he stopped and put his hand to his brow in consternation, as he thought of the elaborate expedition that was being fitted out for the recovery of the treasure.

Prudence, who was sitting in the window reading, looked up at his entrance and smiled.

"Edward Tredgold has been in to see you," she remarked.

The captain nodded. "Couldn't he stop?" he inquired.

"I don't know," said his niece; "I didn't see him. I was upstairs when he came."

Captain Bowers looked perturbed. "Didn't you come down?" he inquired.

"I sent down word that I had a headache," said Miss Drewitt, carelessly.

Despite his sixty odd years the captain turned a little bit pink. "I hope you are better now," he said, at last.

"Oh, yes," said his niece; "it wasn't very bad. It's strange that I should have a headache so soon after you; looks as though they're in the family, doesn't it?"

Somewhat to the captain's relief she took up her book again without waiting for a reply, and sat reading until Mr. Tasker brought in the tea. The captain, who was in a very thoughtful mood, drank cup after cup in silence, and it was not until the meal was cleared away and he had had a few soothing whiffs at his pipe that he narrated the events of the afternoon.

"There!" said Prudence, her eyes sparkling with indignation. "What did I say? Didn't I tell you that those three people would be taking a holiday soon? The idea of Mr. Tredgold venturing to come round here this afternoon!"

"He knows nothing about it," protested the captain.

Miss Drewitt shook her head obstinately. "We shall see," she remarked. "The idea of those men going after your treasure after you had said it wasn't to be touched! Why, it's perfectly dishonest!"

The captain blew a cloud of smoke from his mouth and watched it disperse. "Perhaps they won't find it," he murmured.

"They'll find it," said his niece, confidently. "Why shouldn't they? This Captain Brisket will find the island, and the rest will be easy."

"They might not find the island," said the captain, blowing a cloud so dense that his face was almost hidden. "Some of these little islands have been known to disappear quite suddenly. Volcanic action, you know. What are you smiling at?" he added, sharply.

"Thoughts," said Miss Drewitt, clasping her hands round her knee and smiling again. "I was thinking how odd it would be if the island sank just as they landed upon it."

CHAPTER XII

Mr. Chalk, when half-awake next morning, tried to remember Mr. Stobell's remarks of the night before; fully awake, he tried to forget them. He remembered, too, with a pang that Tredgold had been content to enact the part of a listener, and had made no attempt to check the somewhat unusual fluency of the aggrieved Mr. Stobell. The latter's last instructions were that Mrs. Chalk was to be told, without loss of time, that her presence on the schooner was not to be thought of.

With all this on his mind Mr. Chalk made but a poor breakfast, and his appetite was not improved by his wife's enthusiastic remarks concerning the voyage. Breakfast over, she dispatched a note to Mrs. Stobell by the housemaid, with instructions to wait for a reply. Altogether six notes passed during the morning, and Mr. Chalk, who hazarded a fair notion as to their contents, became correspondingly gloomy.

"We're to go up there at five," said his wife, after reading the last note. "Mr. Stobell will be at tea at that time, and we're to drop in as though by accident."

"What for?" inquired Mr. Chalk, affecting surprise. "Go up where?"

"To talk to Mr. Stobell," said his wife, grimly. "Fancy, poor Mrs. Stobell says that she is sure he won't let her come. I wish he was my husband, that's all."

Mr. Chalk muttered something about "doing a little gardening."

"You can do that another time," said Mrs. Chalk, coldly. "I've noticed you've been very fond of gardening lately."

The allusion was too indirect to contest, but Mr. Chalk reddened despite himself, and his wife, after regarding his confusion with a questioning eye, left him to his own devices and his conscience.

Mr. Stobell and his wife had just sat down to tea when they arrived, and Mrs. Stobell, rising from behind a huge tea-pot, gave a little cry of surprise as her friend entered the room, and kissed her affectionately.

"Well, who would have thought of seeing you?" she cried. "Sit down."

Mrs. Chalk sat down at the large table opposite Mr. Stobell; Mr. Chalk, without glancing in his wife's direction, seated himself by that gentleman's side.

"Well, weren't you surprised?" inquired Mrs. Chalk, loudly, as her hostess passed her a cup of tea.

"Surprised?" said Mrs. Stobell, curiously.

"Why, hasn't Mr. Stobell told you?" exclaimed Mrs. Chalk.

"Told me?" repeated Mrs. Stobell, glancing indignantly at the wide-open eyes of Mr. Chalk. "Told me what?"

It was now Mrs. Chalk's turn to appear surprised, and she did it so well that Mr. Chalk choked in his tea-cup. "About the yachting trip," she said, with a glance at her husband that made his choking take on a ventriloquial effect of distance.

"He—he didn't say anything to me about it," said Mrs. Stobell, timidly.

She glanced at her husband, but Mr. Stobell, taking an enormous bite out of a slice of bread and butter, made no sign.

"It'll do you a world of good," said Mrs. Chalk, affectionately. "It'll put a little colour in your cheeks."

Mrs. Stobell flushed. She was a faded little woman; faded eyes, faded hair, faded cheeks. It was even whispered that her love for Mr. Stobell was beginning to fade.

"And I don't suppose you'll mind the seasickness after you get used to it," said the considerate Mr. Chalk, "and the storms, and the cyclones, and fogs, and collisions, and all that sort of thing."

"If you can stand it, she can," said his wife, angrily.

"But I don't understand," said Mrs. Stobell, appealingly. "What yachting trip?"

Mrs. Chalk began to explain; Mr. Stobell helped himself to another slice, and, except for a single glance under his heavy brows at Mr. Chalk, appeared to be oblivious of his surroundings.

"It sounds very nice," said Mrs. Stobell, after her friend had finished her explanation. "Perhaps it might do me good. I have tried a great many things."

"Mr. Stobell ought to have taken you for a voyage long before," said Mrs. Chalk, with conviction. "Still, better late than never."

"The only thing is," said Mr. Chalk, speaking with an air of great benevolence, "that if the sea didn't suit Mrs. Stobell, she would be unable to get away from it. And, of course, it might upset her very much."

Mr. Stobell wiped some crumbs from his moustache and looked up.

"No, it won't," he said, briefly.

"Is she a good sailor?" queried Mr. Chalk, somewhat astonished at such a remark from that quarter.

"Don't know," said Mr. Stobell, passing his cup up. "But this trip won't upset her—she ain't going."

Mrs. Chalk exclaimed loudly and exchanged glances of consternation with Mrs. Stobell; Mr. Stobell, having explained the position, took some more bread and butter and munched placidly.

"Don't you think it would do her good?" said Mrs. Chalk, at last.

"Might," said Mr. Stobell, slowly, "and then, again, it mightn't."

"But there's no harm in trying," persisted Mrs. Chalk.

Mr. Stobell made no reply. Having reached his fifth slice he was now encouraging his appetite with apricot jam.

"And it's so cheap," continued Mrs. Chalk.

"That's the way I look at it. If she shuts up the house and gets rid of the servants, same as I am going to do, it will save a lot of money."

She glanced at Mr. Stobell, whose slowly working jaws and knitted brows appeared to indicate deep thought, and then gave a slight triumphant nod at his wife.

"Servants are so expensive," she murmured. "Really, I shouldn't be surprised if we saved money on the whole affair. And then think of her health. She has never quite recovered from that attack of bronchitis. She has never looked the same woman since. Think of your feelings if anything happened to her. Nothing would bring her back to you if once she went."

"Went where?" inquired Mr. Stobell, who was not attending very much.

"If she died, I mean," said Mrs. Chalk, shortly.

"We've all got to die some day," said the philosophic Mr. Stobell. "She's forty-six."

Mrs. Stobell interposed. "Not till September, Robert," she said, almost firmly.

"It wouldn't be nice to be buried at sea," remarked Mr. Chalk, contributing his mite to the discussion.

"Of course, it's very impressive; but to be left down there all alone while the ship sails on must be very hard."

Mrs. Stobell's eyes began to get large. "I'm feeling quite well," she gasped.

"Yes, dear," said Mrs. Chalk, with a threatening glance at her husband. "Of course, we know that. But a voyage would do you good. You can't deny that."

Mrs. Stobell, fumbling for her handkerchief, said in a tremulous voice that she had no wish to deny it. Mr. Stobell, appealed to by the energetic Mrs. Chalk, admitted at once that it might do his wife good, but that it wouldn't him.

"We're going to be three jolly bachelors," he declared, and, first nudging Mr. Chalk to attract his attention, deliberately winked at him.

"Oh, indeed!" exclaimed Mrs. Chalk, drawing herself up; "but you forget that I am coming."

"Two jolly bachelors, then," said the undaunted Stobell.

"No," said Mrs. Chalk, shaking her head, "I am not going alone; if Mrs. Stobell can't come I would sooner stay at home."

Mr. Stobell's face cleared; his mouth relaxed and his dull eyes got almost kindly. With the idea of calling the attention of Mr. Chalk to the pleasing results of a little firmness he placed his foot upon that gentleman's toe and bore heavily.

"Best place for you," he said to Mrs. Chalk. "There's no place like home for ladies. You can have each other to tea every day if you like. In fact, there's no reason——" he paused and looked at his wife, half doubtful that he was conceding too much—"there's no reason why you shouldn't sleep at each other's sometimes."

He helped himself to some cake and, rendered polite by good-nature, offered some to Mrs. Chalk.

"Mind, I shall not go unless Mrs. Stobell goes," said the latter, waving the plate away impatiently; "that I am determined upon."

Mr. Chalk, feeling that appearances required it, ventured on a mild—a very mild—remonstrance.

"And he," continued Mrs. Chalk, sternly, indicating her husband with a nod, "doesn't go without me—not a single step, not an inch of the way."

Mr. Chalk collapsed and sat staring at her in dismay. Mr. Stobell, placing both hands on the table, pushed his chair back and eyed her disagreeably.

"It seems to me—" he began.

"I know," said Mrs. Chalk, speaking with some rapidity—"I know just how it seems to you. But that's how it is. If you want my husband to go you have got to have me too, and if you have me you have got to have your wife, and if—"

"What, is there any more of you coming?" demanded Mr. Stobell, with great bitterness.

Mrs. Chalk ignored the question. "*My* husband wouldn't be happy without *me*," she said, primly. "Would you, Thomas?"

"No," said Mr. Chalk, with a gulp.

"We—we're going a long way," said Mr. Stobell, after a long pause.

"Longer the better," retorted Mrs. Chalk.

"We're going among savages," continued Mr. Stobell, casting about for arguments; "cannibal savages."

"They won't eat her," said Mrs. Chalk, with a passing glance at the scanty proportions of her friend, "not while you're about."

"I don't like to take my wife into danger," said Mr. Stobell, with surly bashfulness; "I'm—I'm too fond of her for that. And she don't want to come. Do you, Alice?"

"No," said Mrs. Stobell, dutifully, "but I want to share your dangers, Robert."

"Say 'yes' or 'no' without any trimmings," commanded her husband, as he intercepted a look passing between her and Mrs. Chalk. "Do-you-want-to- come?"

Mrs. Stobell trembled. "I don't want to prevent Mr. Chalk from going," she murmured.

"Never mind about him," said Mr. Stobell.

"*Do—you—want—to—come.*

"Yes," said Mrs. Stobell.

Her husband, hardly able to believe his ears, gazed at her in bewilderment. "Very well, then," he said, in a voice that made the tea-cups rattle. "COME!"

He sat with bent brows gazing at the table as Mrs. Chalk, her face wreathed in triumphant smiles, began to discuss yachting costumes and other necessities of ocean travel with the quivering Mrs. Stobell. Unable to endure it any longer he rose and, in a voice by no means alluring, invited Mr. Chalk into the garden to smoke a pipe; Mr. Chalk, helping himself to two pieces of cake as evidence, said that he had not yet finished his tea. Owing partly to lack of appetite and partly to the face which Mr. Stobell pressed to the window every other minute to entice him out, he made but slow progress.

The matter was discussed next day as they journeyed down to Biddlecombe with Mr. Tredgold to complete the purchase of the schooner, the views of the latter gentleman coinciding so exactly with those of Mr. Stobell that Mr. Chalk was compelled to listen to the same lecture twice.

Under this infliction his spirits began to droop, nor did they revive until, from the ferry-boat, his eyes fell upon the masts of the *Fair Emily,* and the trim figure of Captain Brisket standing at the foot of the steps awaiting their arrival.

"We've had a stroke of good luck, gentlemen," said Brisket, in a husky whisper, as they followed him up the steps. "See that man?"

He pointed to a thin, dismal-looking man, standing a yard or two away, who was trying to appear unconscious of their scrutiny.

"Peter Duckett," said Brisket, in the same satisfied whisper.

Mr. Stobell, ever willing for a free show, stared at the dismal man and groped in the recesses of his memory. The name seemed familiar.

"The man who ate three dozen hard-boiled eggs in four minutes?" he asked, with a little excitement natural in the circumstances.

Captain Brisket stared at him. "No; Peter Duckett, the finest mate that ever sailed," he said, with a flourish. "We're lucky to have the chance of getting him, I can tell you. To see him handle sailormen is a revelation; to see him handle a ship—"

He broke off and shook his head with the air of a man who despaired of doing justice to his subject. "These are the gentlemen, Peter," he said, introducing them with a wave of his hand.

Mr. Duckett raised his cap, and tugging at a small patch of reddish-brown hair strangely resembling a door-mat in texture, which grew at the base of his chin, cleared his throat and said it was a fine morning.

"Not much of a talker is Peter," said the genial Brisket. "He's a doer; that's what he is-a doer. Now, if you're willing—and I hope you are— he'll come aboard with us and talk the matter over."

This proposition being assented to after a little delay on the part of Mr. Stobell, who appeared to think Mr. Duckett's lack of connection with the hard-boiled eggs somewhat suspicious, they proceeded to Todd's Wharf and made a thorough inspection of the schooner. Mr. Chalk's eyes grew bright and his step elastic. He roamed from forecastle to cabin and from cabin to galley, and, his practice with the crow's-nest in Dialstone Lane standing him in good stead, wound up by ascending to the masthead and waving to his astonished friends below.

Mr. Todd came on board as he regained the deck, and, stroking his white beard, regarded him with an air of benevolent interest.

"There's no ill-feeling," he said, as Mr. Chalk eyed his outstretched hand somewhat dubiously. "You're a hard nut, that's what you are, and I pity anybody that has the cracking of you. A man that could come and offer me seventy pounds for a craft like this—seventy pounds, mind you," he added, with a rising colour, as he turned to the others "seventy pounds, and a face like a baby. Why, when I think of it, DAMME IF I DON'T—"

Captain Brisket laid his hand on his arm and with soothing words led him below. His voice was heard booming in the cabin until at length it ended in a roar of laughter, and Captain Brisket, appearing at the companion, beckoned them below, with a whispered injunction to Mr. Chalk to keep as much in the background as possible.

The business was soon concluded, and Mr. Chalk's eye brightened again as he looked on his new property. Captain Brisket, in high good-humour, began to talk of accommodation, and, among other things, suggested a scheme of cutting through the bulkhead at the foot of the companion- ladder and building a commodious cabin with three berths in the hold.

"There are two ladies coming," said Mr. Chalk.

Captain Brisket rubbed his chin. "I'd forgotten that," he said, slowly. "Two, did you say?"

"It doesn't matter," said Mr. Stobell, fixing him with his left eye and slowly veiling the right. "You go on with them alterations. One of the ladies can have your state-room and the other the mate's bunk."

"Where are Captain Brisket and the mate to sleep?" inquired Mr. Chalk.

"Anywhere," replied Mr. Stobell. "With the crew if they like."

Captain Brisket, looking suddenly very solemn, shook his head and said that it was impossible. He spoke in moving terms of the danger to discipline, and called upon Mr. Duckett to confirm his fears. Meantime, Mr. Stobell, opening his right eye slowly, winked with the left.

"You go on with them alterations," he repeated.

Captain Brisket started and reflected. A nod from Mr. Tredgold and a significant gesture in the direction of the unconscious Mr. Chalk decided him. "Very good, gentlemen," he said, cheerfully. "I'm in your hands, and Peter Ducket'll do what I do. It's settled he's coming, I suppose?"

Mr. Tredgold, after a long look at the anxious face of Mr. Duckett, said "Yes," and then at Captain Brisket's suggestion the party adjourned to the Jack Ashore, where in a little room upstairs, not much larger than the schooner's cabin, the preparations for the voyage were discussed in detail.

"And mind, Peter," said Captain Brisket to his friend, as the pair strolled along by the harbour after their principals had departed, "the less you say about this the better. We don't want any Biddlecombe men in it."

"Why not?" inquired the other.

"Because," replied Brisket, lowering his voice, "there's more in this than meets the eye. They're not the sort to go on a cruise to the islands for pleasure—except Chalk, that is. I've been keeping my ears open, and there's something afoot. D'ye take me?"

Mr. Duckett nodded shrewdly.

"I'll pick a crew for 'em," said Brisket. "A man here and a man there. Biddlecombe men ain't tough enough. And now, what about that whisky you've been talking so much about?"

CHAPTER XIII

Further secrecy as to the projected trip being now useless, Mr. Tredgold made the best of the situation and talked freely concerning it. To the astonished Edward he spoke feelingly of seeing the world before the insidious encroachments of age should render it impossible; to Captain Bowers, whom he met in the High Street, he discussed destinations with the air of a man whose mind was singularly open on the subject. If he had any choice it appeared that it was in the direction of North America.

"You might do worse," said the captain, grimly.

"Chalk," said Mr. Tredgold, meditatively "Chalk favours the South. I think that he got rather excited by your description of the islands there. He is a very—"

"If you are going to try and find that island I spoke about," interrupted the captain, impatiently, "I warn you solemnly that you are wasting both your time and your money. If I had known of this voyage I would have told you so before. If you take my advice you'll sell your schooner and stick to business you understand."

Mr. Tredgold laughed easily. "We may look for it if we go that way," he said. "I believe that Chalk has bought a trowel, in case we run up against it. He has got a romantic belief in coincidences, you know."

"Very good," said the captain, turning away. "Only don't blame me, whatever happens. You can't say I have not warned you."

He clutched his stick by the middle and strode off down the road. Mr. Tredgold, gazing after his retreating figure with a tolerant smile, wondered whether he would take his share of the treasure when it was offered to him.

The anxiety of Miss Vickers at this period was intense. Particulars of the purchase of the schooner were conveyed to her by letter, but the feminine desire of talking the matter over with somebody became too strong to be denied. She even waylaid Mr. Stobell one evening, and, despite every discouragement, insisted upon walking part of the way home with him. He sat for hours afterwards recalling the tit-bits of a summary of his personal charms with which she had supplied him.

Mr. Chalk spent the time in preparations for the voyage, purchasing, among other necessaries, a stock of firearms of all shapes and sizes, with which he practised in the garden. Most marksmen diminish gradually the size of their target; but Mr. Chalk, after starting with a medicine-bottle at a hundred yards, wound up with the greenhouse at fifteen. Mrs. Chalk, who was inside at the time tending an invalid geranium, acted as marker, and, although Mr. Chalk proved by actual measurement that the bullet had not gone within six inches of her, the range was closed.

By the time the alterations on the *Fair Emily* were finished the summer was nearly at an end, and it was not until the 20th of August that the travellers met on Binchester platform. Mrs. Chalk, in a smart yachting costume, with a white-peaked cap, stood by a pile of luggage discoursing to an admiring circle of friends who had come to see her off. She had shut up her house and paid off her servants, and her pity for Mrs. Stobell, whose husband had forbidden such a course in her case, provided a suitable and agreeable subject for conversation. Mrs. Stobell had economised in quite a different direction, and Mrs. Chalk gazed in indignant pity at the one small box and the Gladstone bag which contained her wardrobe.

"She don't want to dress up on shipboard," said Mr. Stobell.

Mrs. Chalk turned and eyed her friend's costume—a plain tweed coat and skirt, in which she had first appeared the spring before last.

"If we're away a year," she said, decidedly, "she'll be in rags before we get back."

Mr. Stobell said that fortunately they would be in a warm climate, and turned to greet the Tredgolds, who had just arrived. Then the train came in, and Mr. Chalk, appearing suddenly from behind the luggage, where he had been standing since he had first caught sight of the small, anxious face of Selina Vickers on the platform, entered the carriage and waved cheery adieus to Binchester.

To the eyes of Mr. Chalk and his wife Biddlecombe appeared to have put on holiday attire for the occasion. With smiling satisfaction they led the way to the ferry, Mrs. Chalk's costume exciting so much attention that the remainder of the party hung behind to watch Edward Tredgold fasten his bootlace. It took two boats to convey the luggage to the schooner, and the cargo of the smaller craft shifting in mid-stream, the boatman pulled the remainder of the way with a large portion of it in his lap. Unfortunately, his mouth was free.

Mr. Chalk could not restrain a cry of admiration as he clambered on board the *Fair Emily*. The deck was as white as that of a man-of-war, and her brass-work twinkled in the sun. White paint work and the honest and healthy smell of tar completed his satisfaction. His chest expanded as he sniffed the breeze, and with a slight nautical roll paced up and down the spotless deck.

"And now," said Captain Brisket, after a couple of sturdy seamen had placed the men's luggage in the new cabin, "which of you ladies is going to have my state-room, and which the mate's bunk?"

Mrs. Chalk started; she had taken it for granted that she was to have the state-room. She turned and eyed her friend anxiously.

"The bunk seems to get the most air," said Mrs. Stobell. "And it's nearer the ladder in case of emergencies."

"You have it, dear," said Mrs. Chalk, tenderly. "I'm not nervous."

"But you are so fond of fresh air," said Mrs. Stobell, with a longing glance at the state-room. "I don't like to be selfish."

"You're not," said Mrs. Chalk, with conviction.

"Chalk and I will toss for it," said Mr. Stobell, who had been listening with some impatience. He spun a coin in the air, and Mr. Chalk, winning the bunk for his indignant wife, was at some pains to dilate upon its manifold advantages. Mrs. Stobell, with a protesting smile, had her things carried into the state-room, while Mrs. Chalk stood by listening coldly to plans for putting her heavy luggage in the hold.

"What time do we start?" inquired Tredgold senior, moving towards the companion-ladder.

"Four o'clock, sir," replied Brisket.

Mr. Stobell, his heavy features half-lit by an unwonted smile, turned and surveyed his friends. "I've ordered a little feed at the King of Hanover at half-past one," he said, awkwardly. "We'll be back on board by half-past three, captain."

Captain Brisket bowed, and the party were making preparations for departure when a hitch was caused by the behaviour of Mrs. Chalk, who was still brooding over the affair of the state-room. In the plainest of plain terms she declared that she did not want any luncheon and preferred to stay on board. Her gloom seemed to infect the whole party, Mr. Stobell in particular being so dejected that his wife eyed him in amazement.

"It'll spoil it for all of us if you don't come," he said, with bashful surliness. "Why, I arranged the lunch more for you than anybody. It'll be our last meal on shore."

Mrs. Chalk said that she had had so many meals on shore that she could afford to miss one, and Mr. Stobell, after eyeing her for some time in a manner strangely at variance with his words, drew his wife to one side and whispered fiercely in her ear.

"Well, I sha'n't go without her," said Mrs. Stobell, rejoining the group. "What with losing that nice, airy bunk and getting that nasty, stuffy stateroom, I don't feel like eating."

Mrs. Chalk's countenance cleared. "Don't you like it, dear?" she said, affectionately. "Change, by all means, if you don't. Never mind about their stupid tossing."

Mrs. Stobell changed, and Mr. Tredgold senior, after waiting a decent interval for the sake of appearances, entreated both ladies to partake of the luncheon. Unable to resist any longer, Mrs. Chalk gave way, and in the ship's boat, propelled by the brawny arms of two of the crew, went ashore with the others.

Luncheon was waiting for them in the coffee-room of the inn, and the table was brave with flowers and bottles of champagne. Impressed by the occasion George the waiter attended upon them with unusual decorum, and the landlady herself entered the room two or three times to see that things were proceeding properly.

"Here's to our next meal on shore," said Mr. Chalk, raising his glass and nodding solemnly at Edward.

"That will be tea for me," said the latter. "I shall come back here, I expect, and take a solitary cup to your memory. Let me have a word as soon as you can."

"You ought to get a cable from Sydney in about six or seven months," said his father.

His son nodded. "Don't trouble about any expressions of affection," he urged; "they'd come expensive. If you find me dead of overwork when you come back——"

"I shall contest the certificate," said his father, with unwonted frivolity.

"I wonder how we shall sleep to-night?" said Mrs. Stobell, with a little shiver. "Fancy, only a few planks between us and the water!"

"That won't keep me awake," said Mrs. Chalk, decidedly; "but I shouldn't sleep a wink if I had left my girls in the house, the same as you have. I should lie awake all night wondering what tricks they'd be up to."

"But you've left your house unprotected," said Mrs. Stobell.

"The house won't run away," retorted her friend, "and I've sent all my valuables to the bank and to friends to take care of, and had all my carpets taken up and beaten and warehoused. I can't imagine what Mr. Stobell was thinking of not to let you do the same."

"There's a lot as would like to know what I'm thinking of sometimes," remarked Mr. Stobell, with a satisfied air.

Mrs. Chalk glanced at him superciliously, but, remembering that he was her host, refrained from the only comments she felt to be suitable to the occasion. Under the tactful guidance of Edward Tredgold the conversation was led to shipwrecks, fires at sea, and other subjects of the kind comforting to the landsman, Mr. Chalk favouring them with a tale of a giant octopus, culled from Captain Bowers's collection, which made Mrs. Stobell's eyes dilate with horror.

"You won't see any octopuses," said her husband. "You needn't worry about them."

He got up from the table, and crossing to the window stood with his hands behind his back, smoking one of the "King of Hanover's" cigars.

"Very good smoke this," he said, taking the cigar from his mouth and inspecting it critically. "I think I'll take a box or two with me."

"Just what I was thinking," said Mr. Jasper Tredgold. "Let's go down and see the landlord."

Mr. Stobell followed him slowly from the room, leaving Mr. Chalk and Edward to entertain the ladies. The former gentleman, clad in a neat serge suit, an open collar, and a knotted necktie, leaned back in his chair, puffing contentedly at one of the cigars which had excited the encomiums of his friends. He was just about to help himself to a little, more champagne when Mr. Stobell, reappearing at the door, requested him to come and give them the benefit of his opinion in the matter of cigars.

"They don't seem up to sample," he said, with a growl; "and you're a good judge of a cigar."

Mr. Chalk rose and followed him downstairs, where, to his great astonishment, he was at once seized by Mr. Tredgold and led outside.

"Anything wrong?" he demanded.

"We must get to the ship at once," said Tredgold, in an excited whisper. "*The men!*"

Mr. Chalk, much startled, clapped his hands to his head and spoke of going back for his hat.

"Never mind about your hat," said Stobell, impatiently; "we haven't got ours either."

He took Mr. Chalk's other arm and started off at a rapid pace.

"What is the matter?" inquired Mr. Chalk, looking from one to the other.

"Message from Captain Brisket to go on board at once, or he won't be answerable for the consequences," replied Tredgold, in a thrilling whisper; "and, above all, to bring Mr. Chalk to quiet the men."

Mr. Chalk turned a ghastly white. "Is it mutiny?" he faltered. "Already?"

"Something o' the sort," said Stobell.

Despite his friend's great strength, Mr. Chalk for one moment almost brought him to a standstill. Then, in a tremulous voice, he spoke of going to the police.

"We don't want the police," said Tredgold, sharply. "If you're afraid, Chalk, you'd better go back and stay with the ladies while we settle the affair."

Mr. Chalk flushed, and holding his head erect said no more. Mr. Duckett and a waterman were waiting for them at the stairs, and, barely giving them time to jump in, pushed off and pulled with rapid strokes to the schooner. Mr. Chalk's heart failed him as they drew near and he saw men moving rapidly about her deck. His last thoughts as he clambered over the side were of his wife.

In blissful ignorance of his proceedings, Mrs. Chalk, having adjusted her cap in the glass and drawn on her gloves, sat patiently awaiting his return. She even drew a good-natured comparison between the time spent on choosing cigars and bonnets.

"There's plenty of time," she said, in reply to an uneasy remark of Mrs. Stobell's. "It's only just three, and we don't sail until four. What is that horrid, clanking noise?"

"Some craft getting up her anchor," said Edward, going to the window and leaning out. "WHY! HALLOA!"

"What's the matter?" said both ladies.

Edward drew in his head and regarded them with an expression of some bewilderment.

"It's the *Fair Emily*," he said, slowly, "and she's hoisting her sails."

"Just trying the machinery to see that it's all right, I suppose," said Mrs. Chalk. "My husband said that Captain Brisket is a very careful man."

Edward Tredgold made no reply. He glanced first at three hats standing in a row on the sideboard, and then at the ladies as they came to the window, and gazed with innocent curiosity at the schooner. Even as they looked she drew slowly ahead, and a boat piled up with luggage, which had been lying the other side of her, became visible. Mrs. Chalk gazed at it in stupefaction.

"It can't be ours," she gasped. "They—they'd never dare! They—they—"

She stood for a moment staring at the hats on the sideboard, and then, followed by the others, ran hastily downstairs. There was a hurried questioning of the astonished landlady, and then, Mrs. Chalk leading, they made their way to the stairs at a pace remarkable in a woman of her age and figure. Mrs. Stobell, assisted by Edward Tredgold, did her best to keep up with her, but she reached the goal some distance ahead, and, jumping heavily into a boat, pointed to the fast-receding schooner and bade the boatman overtake it.

"Can't be done, ma'am," said the man, staring, "not without wings."

"Row hard," said Mrs. Chalk, in a voice of sharp encouragement.

The boatman, a man of few words, jerked his thumb in the direction of the *Fair Emily,* which was already responding to the motion of the sea outside.

"You run up the road on to them cliffs and wave to'em," he said, slowly. "Wave 'ard."

Mrs. Chalk hesitated, and then, stepping out of the boat, resumed the pursuit by land. Ten minutes' hurried walking brought them to the cliffs, and standing boldly on the verge she enacted, to the great admiration of a small crowd, the part of a human semaphore.

The schooner, her bows pointing gradually seawards, for some time made no sign. Then a little group clustered at the stern and waved farewells.

CHAPTER XIV

Mrs. Chalk watched the schooner until it was a mere white speck on the horizon, a faint idea that it might yet see the error of its ways and return for her chaining her to the spot. Compelled at last to recognise the inevitable, she rose from the turf on which she had been sitting and, her face crimson with wrath, denounced husbands in general and her own in particular.

"It's my husband's doing, I'm sure," said Mrs. Stobell, with a side glance at her friend's attire, not entirely devoid of self- congratulation. "That's why he wouldn't let me have a yachting costume. I can see it now."

Mrs. Chalk turned and eyed her with angry disdain.

"And that's why he wouldn't let me bring more than one box," continued Mrs. Stobell, with the air of one to whom all things had been suddenly revealed; "and why he wouldn't shut the house up. Oh, just fancy what a pickle I should have been in if I had! I must say it was thoughtful of him."

"*Thoughtful!*" exclaimed Mrs. Chalk, in a choking voice.

"And I ought to have suspected something," continued Mrs. Stobell, "because he kissed me this morning. I can see now that he meant it for goodbye! Well, I can't say I'm surprised. Robert always does get his own way."

"If you hadn't persuaded me to come ashore for that wretched luncheon," said Mrs. Chalk, in a deep voice, "we should have been all right."

"I'm sure I wasn't to know," said her friend, "although I certainly thought it odd when Robert said that he had got it principally for you. I could see you were a little bit flattered."

Mrs. Chalk, trembling with anger, sought in vain for a retort.

"Well, it's no good staying here," said Mrs. Stobell, philosophically. "We had better get home."

"*Home!*" cried Mrs. Chalk, as a vision of her bare floors and dismantled walls rose before her. "When I think of the deceitfulness of those men, giving us champagne and talking about the long evenings on board, I don't know what to do with myself. And your father was one of them," she added, turning suddenly upon Edward.

Mr. Tredgold disowned his erring parent with some haste, and, being by this time rather tired of the proceedings, suggested that they should return to the inn and look up trains—a proposal to which Mrs. Chalk, after a final glance seawards, silently assented. With head erect she led the way down to the town again, her bearing being so impressive that George the waiter, who had been watching for them, after handing her a letter which had been entrusted to him, beat a precipitate retreat.

The letter, which was from Mr. Stobell, was short and to the point. It narrated the artifice by which Mr. Chalk had been lured away, and concluded with a general statement that women were out of place on shipboard. This, Mrs. Stobell declared, after perusing the letter, was intended for an apology.

Mrs. Chalk received the information in stony silence, and, declining tea, made her way to the station and mounted guard over her boxes until the train was due. With the exception of saying "Indeed!" on three or four occasions she kept silent all the way to Binchester, and, arrived there, departed for home in a cab, in spite of a most pressing invitation from Mrs. Stobell to stay with her until her own house was habitable.

Mr. Tredgold parted from them both with relief. The voyage had been a source of wonder to him from its first inception, and the day's proceedings had only served to increase the mystery. He made a light supper and, the house being too quiet for his taste, went for a meditative stroll. The shops were closed and the small thoroughfares almost deserted. He wondered whether it was too late to call and talk over the affair with Captain Bowers, and, still wondering, found himself in Dialstone Lane.

Two or three of the houses were in darkness, but there was a cheerful light behind the drawn blind of the captain's sitting-room. He hesitated a moment and then rapped lightly on the door, and no answer being forthcoming rapped again. The door opened and revealed the amiable features of Mr. Tasker.

"Captain Bowers has gone to London, sir," he said.

Mr. Tredgold drew his right foot back three inches, and at the same time tried to peer into the room.

"We're expecting him back every moment," said Mr. Tasker, encouragingly.

Mr. Tredgold moved his foot forward again and pondered. "It's very late, but I wanted to see him rather particularly," he murmured, as he stepped into the room.

"Miss Drewitt's in the garden," said Joseph.

Mr. Tredgold started and eyed him suspiciously. Mr. Tasker's face, however, preserving its usual appearance of stolid simplicity, his features relaxed and he became thoughtful again.

"Perhaps I might go into the garden," he suggested.

"I should if I was you, sir," said Joseph, preceding him and throwing open the back door. "It's fresher out there."

Mr. Tredgold stepped into the garden and stood blinking in the sudden darkness. There was no moon and the night was cloudy, a fact which accounted for his unusual politeness towards a cypress of somewhat stately bearing which stood at one corner of the small lawn. He replaced his hat hastily, and an apologetic remark concerning the lateness of his visit was never finished. A trifle confused, he walked down the garden, peering right and left as he went, but without finding the object of his search. Twice he paced the garden from end to end, and he had just arrived at the conclusion that Mr. Tasker had made a mistake when a faint sound high above his head apprised him of the true state of affairs.

He stood listening in amazement, but the sound was not repeated. Ordinary prudence and a sense of the fitness of things suggested that he should go home; inclination suggested that he should seat himself in the deck-chair at the foot of the crow's-nest and await events. He sat down to consider the matter.

Sprawling comfortably in the chair he lit his pipe, his ear on the alert to catch the slightest sound of the captive in the cask above. The warm air was laden with the scent of flowers, and nothing stirred with the exception of Mr. Tasker's shadow on the blind of the kitchen window. The clock in the neighbouring church chimed the three-quarters, and in due time boomed out the hour of ten. Mr. Tredgold knocked the ashes from his pipe and began seriously to consider his position. Lights went out in the next house. Huge shadows appeared on the kitchen blind and the light gradually faded, to reappear triumphantly in the room above. Anon the shadow of Mr. Tasker's head was seen wrestling fiercely with its back collar-stud.

"Mr. Tredgold!" said a sharp voice from above.

Mr. Tredgold sprang to his feet, overturning the chair in his haste, and gazed aloft.

"Miss Drewitt!" he cried, in accents of intense surprise.

"I am coming down," said the voice.

"Pray be careful," said Mr. Tredgold, anxiously; "it is very dark. Can I help you?"

"Yes—you can go indoors," said Miss Drewitt.

Her tone was so decided and so bitter that Mr. Tredgold, merely staying long enough to urge extreme carefulness in the descent, did as he was desired. He went into the sitting-room and, standing uneasily by the fireplace, tried to think out his line of action. He was still floundering when he heard swift footsteps coming up the garden, and Miss Drewitt, very upright and somewhat flushed of face, confronted him.

"I—I called to see the captain," he said, hastily, "and Joseph told me you were in the garden. I couldn't see you anywhere, so I took the liberty of sitting out there to wait for the captain's return."

Miss Drewitt listened impatiently. "Did you know that I was up in the crow's-nest?" she demanded.

"Joseph never said a word about it," said Mr. Tredgold, with an air of great frankness. "He merely said that you were in the garden, and, not being able to find you, I thought that he was mistaken."

"Did you know that I was up in the crow's-nest?" repeated Miss Drewitt, with ominous persistency.

"A—a sort of idea that you might be there did occur to me after a time," admitted the other.

"Did you know that I was there?"

Mr. Tredgold gazed at her in feeble indignation, but the uselessness of denial made truth easier. "Yes," he said, slowly.

"Thank you," said the girl, scornfully. "You thought that I shouldn't like to be caught up there, and that it would be an amusing and gentlemanly thing to do to keep me a prisoner. I quite understand. My estimate of you has turned out to be correct."

"It was quite an accident," urged Mr. Tredgold, humbly. "I've had a very worrying day seeing them off at Biddlecombe, and when I heard you up in the nest I succumbed to sudden temptation. If I had stopped to think—if I had had the faintest idea that you would catechise me in the way you have done—I shouldn't have dreamt of doing such a thing."

Miss Drewitt, who was standing with her hand on the latch of the door leading upstairs, as a hint that the interview was at an end, could not restrain her indignation.

"Your father and his friends have gone off to secure my uncle's treasure, and you come straight on here," she cried, hotly. "Do you think that there is no end to his good-nature?"

"Treasure?" said the other, with a laugh. "Why, that idea was knocked on the head when the map was burnt. Even Chalk wouldn't go on a roving commission to dig over all the islands in the South Pacific."

"I don't see anything to laugh at," said the girl; "my uncle fully intended to burn it. He was terribly upset when he found that it had disappeared."

"Disappeared?" cried Mr. Tredgold, in accents of unmistakable amazement. "Why, wasn't it burnt after all? The captain said it was."

"He was going to burn it," repeated the girl, watching him; "but somebody took it from the bureau."

"Took it? When?" inquired the other, as the business of the yachting cruise began to appear before him in its true colours.

"The afternoon you were here waiting for him," said Miss Drewitt.

"Afternoon?" repeated Mr. Tredgold, blankly. "The afternoon I was——" He drew himself up and eyed her angrily. "Do you mean to say that you think I took the thing?"

"It doesn't matter what I think," said the girl. "I suppose you won't deny that your friends have got it?"

"Yes; but you said that it was the afternoon I was here," persisted the other.

Miss Drewitt eyed him indignantly. The conscience-stricken culprit of a few minutes before had disappeared, leaving in his stead an arrogant young man, demanding explanations in a voice of almost unbecoming loudness.

"You are shouting at me," she said, stiffly.

Mr. Tredgold apologised, but returned to the charge. "I answered your question a little while ago," he said, in more moderate tones; "now, please, answer mine. Do you think that I took the map?"

"I am not to be commanded to speak by you," said Miss Drewitt, standing very erect.

"Fair-play is a jewel," said the other. "Question for question. Do you?"

Miss Drewitt looked at him and hesitated. "No," she said, at last, with obvious reluctance.

Mr. Tredgold's countenance cleared and his eyes softened.

"I suppose you admit that your father has got it?" said the girl, noting these signs with some disapproval. "How did he get it?"

Mr. Tredgold shook his head. "If those three overgrown babes find that treasure," he said, impressively, "I'll doom myself to perpetual bachelorhood."

"I answered your question just now," said the girl, very quietly, "because I wanted to ask you one. Do you believe my uncle's story about the buried treasure?"

Mr. Tredgold eyed her uneasily. "I never attached much importance to it," he replied. "It seemed rather romantic."

"Do you believe it?"

"No," said the other, doggedly.

The girl drew a long breath and favoured him with a look in which triumph and anger were strangely mingled.

"I wonder you can visit him after thinking him capable of such a falsehood," she said, at last. "You certainly won't be able to after I have told him."

"I told you in confidence," was the reply. "I have regarded it all along as a story told to amuse Chalk; that is all. I shall be very sorry if you say anything that might cause unpleasantness between myself and Captain Bowers."

"I shall tell him as soon as he comes in," said Miss Drewitt. "It is only right that he should know your opinion of him. Good-night."

Mr. Tredgold said "good-night," and, walking to the door, stood for a moment regarding her thoughtfully. It was quite clear that in her present state of mind any appeal to her better nature would be worse than useless. He resolved to try the effect of a little humility.

"I am very sorry for my behaviour in the garden," he said, sorrowfully.

"It doesn't matter," said the girl; "I wasn't at all surprised."

Mr. Tredgold recognised the failure of the new treatment at once. "Of course, when I went into the garden I hadn't any idea that you would be in such an unlikely place," he said, with a kindly smile. "Let us hope that you won't go there again."

Miss Drewitt, hardly able to believe her ears, let him go without a word, and in a dazed fashion stood at the door and watched him up the lane. When the captain came in a little later she was sitting in a stiff and uncomfortable attitude by the window, still thinking.

He was so tired after a long day in town that the girl, at considerable personal inconvenience, allowed him to finish his supper before recounting the manifold misdeeds of Mr. Tredgold. She waited until he had pushed his chair back and lit a pipe, and then without any preface plunged into the subject with an enthusiasm which she endeavoured in vain to make contagious. The captain listened in silence and turned a somewhat worried face in her direction when she had finished.

"We can't all think alike," he said, feebly, as she waited with flushed cheeks and sparkling eyes for the verdict. "I told you he hadn't taken the map. As for those three idiots and their harebrained voyage—"

"But Mr. Tredgold said that he didn't believe in the treasure," said the wrathful Prudence. "One thing is, he can never come here again; I think that I made him understand that. The idea of thinking that you could tell a falsehood!"

The captain bent down and, picking a used match from the hearthrug, threw it carefully under the grate. Miss Drewitt watched him expectantly.

"We mustn't quarrel with people's opinions," he said, at last. "It's a free country, and people can believe what they like. Look at Protestants and Catholics, for instance; their belief isn't the same, and yet I've known 'em to be staunch friends."

Miss Drewitt shook her head. "He can never come here again," she said, with great determination. "He has insulted you, and if you were not the best-natured man in the world you would be as angry about it as I am."

The captain smoked in silence.

"And his father and those other two men will come back with your treasure," continued Prudence, after waiting for some time for him to speak. "And, so far as I can see, you won't even be able to prosecute them for it."

"I sha'n't do anything," said Captain Bowers, impatiently, as he rose and knocked out his half-smoked pipe, "and I never want to hear another word about that treasure as long as I live. I'm tired of it. It has caused more mischief and unpleasantness than—than it is worth. They are welcome to it for me."

CHAPTER XV

Mr. Chalk's foot had scarcely touched the deck of the schooner when Mr. Tredgold seized him by the arm and, whispering indistinctly in his ear, hurried him below.

"Get your arms out of the cabin as quick as you can," he said, sharply. "Then follow me up on deck."

Mr. Chalk, trembling violently, tried to speak, but in vain. A horrid clanking noise sounded overhead, and with the desperation of terror he turned into the new cabin and, collecting his weapons, began with frantic haste to load them. Then he dropped his rifle and sprang forward with a loud cry as he heard the door close smartly and the key turn in the lock.

He stood gazing stupidly at the door and listening to the noise overhead. The clanking ceased, and was succeeded by a rush of heavy feet, above which he heard Captain Brisket shouting hoarsely. He threw a despairing glance around his prison, and then looked up at the skylight. It was not big enough to crawl through, but he saw that by standing on the table he could get his head out. No less clearly he saw how easy it would be for a mutineer to hit it.

Huddled up in a corner of the cabin he tried to think. Tredgold and Stobell were strangely silent, and even the voice of Brisket had ceased. The suspense became unbearable. Then suddenly a faint creaking and straining of timbers apprised him of the fact that the Fair Emily was under way.

He sprang to his feet and beat heavily upon the door, but it was of stout wood and opened inwards. Then a bright idea, the result of reading sensational fiction, occurred to him, and raising his rifle to his shoulder he aimed at the lock and pulled the trigger.

The noise of the explosion in the small cabin was deafening, but, loud as it was, it failed to drown a cry of alarm outside. The sound of heavy feet and of two or three bodies struggling for precedence up the companion-ladder followed, and Mr. Chalk, still holding his smoking rifle and regarding a splintered hole in the centre of the panel, wondered whether he had hit anybody. He slipped in a fresh cartridge and, becoming conscious of a partial darkening of the skylight, aimed hastily at a face which appeared there. The face, which bore a strong resemblance to that of Mr. Stobell, disappeared with great suddenness.

"He's gone clean off his head," said Captain Brisket, as Mr. Stobell staggered back.

"Mad as a March hare," said Mr. Tredgold, shivering; "it's a wonder he didn't have one of us just now. Call down to him that it's all right, Stobell."

"Call yourself," said that gentleman, shortly.

"Get a stick and raise the skylight," said Tredgold.

A loud report sounded from below. Mr. Chalk had fired a second and successful shot at the lock. "What's he doing?" inquired Stobell, blankly.

A sharp exclamation from Captain Brisket was the only reply, and he turned just as Mr. Chalk, with a rifle in one hand and a revolver in the other, appeared on deck. The captain's cry was echoed forward, and three of the crew dived with marvellous skill into the forecastle. The boy and two others dashed into the galley so hurriedly that the cook, who was peeping out, was borne backwards on to the stove and kept there, the things he said in the heat of the moment being attributed to excitement and attracting no attention. Tredgold, Brisket, and Stobell dodged behind the galley, and Mr. Chalk was left to gaze in open-mouthed wonder at the shrinking figure of Mr. Duckett at the wheel. They regarded each other in silence, until a stealthy step behind Mr. Chalk made him turn round smartly. Mr. Stobell, who was stealing up to secure him, dodged hastily behind the mainmast.

"Stobell!" cried Mr. Chalk, faintly.

"It's all right," said the other.

Mr. Chalk regarded his proceedings in amazement. "What are you hiding behind the mast for?" he inquired, stepping towards him.

Mr. Stobell made no reply, but with an agility hardly to be expected of one of his bulk dashed behind the galley again.

A sense of mystery and unreality stole over Mr. Chalk. He began to think that he must be dreaming. He turned and looked at Mr. Duckett, and Mr. Duckett, trying to smile at him, contorted his face so horribly that he shrank back appalled. He looked about him and saw that they were now in open water and drawing gradually away from the land. The stillness and mystery became unbearable, and with an air of resolution he cocked his rifle and proceeded with infinite caution to stalk the galley. As he weathered it, with his finger on the trigger, Stobell and the others stole round the other side and, making a mad break aft, stumbled down the companion-ladder and secured themselves below.

"Has everybody gone mad?" inquired Mr. Chalk, approaching the mate again.

"Everybody except you, sir," said Mr. Duckett, with great politeness.

Mr. Chalk looked forward again and nearly dropped his rifle as he saw three or four tousled heads protruding from the galley. Instinctively he took a step towards Mr. Duckett, and instinctively that much-enduring man threw up his hands and cried to him not to shoot. Mr. Chalk, pale of face and trembling of limb, strove to reassure him.

"But it's pointing towards me," said the mate, "and you've got your finger on the trigger."

Mr. Chalk apologized.

"What did Tredgold and Stobell run away for?" he demanded.

Mr. Duckett said that perhaps they were—like himself—nervous of firearms. He also, in reply to further questions, assured him that the mutiny was an affair of the past, and, gaining confidence, begged him to hold the wheel steady for a moment. Mr. Chalk, still clinging to his weapons, laid hold of it, and the mate, running to the companion, called to those below. Led by Mr. Stobell they came on deck.

"It's all over now," said Tredgold, soothingly.

"As peaceable as lambs," said Captain Brisket, taking a gentle hold of the rifle, while Stobell took the revolver.

Mr. Chalk smiled faintly, and then looked round in trepidation as the inmates of the galley drew near and scowled at him curiously.

"Get for'ard!" cried Brisket, turning on them sharply. "Keep your own end o' the ship. D'ye hear?"

The men shuffled off slowly, keeping a wary eye on Mr. Chalk as they went, the knowledge of the tempting mark offered by their backs to an eager sportsman being apparent to all.

"It's all over," said Brisket, taking the wheel from the mate and motioning to him to go away, "and after your determination, sir, there'll be no more of it, I'm sure."

"But what was it?" demanded Mr. Chalk. "Mutiny?"

"Not exactly what you could call mutiny," replied the captain, in a low voice. "A little mistake o' Duckett's. He's a nervous man, and perhaps he exaggerated a little. But don't allude to it again, for the sake of his feelings."

"But somebody locked me in the cabin," persisted Mr. Chalk, looking from one to the other.

Captain Brisket hesitated. "Did they?" he said, with a smile of perplexity. "Did they? I gave orders that that door was to be kept locked when there was nobody in there, and I expect the cook did it by mistake as he passed. It's been a chapter of accidents all through, but I must say, sir, that the determined way you came on deck was wonderful."

"Extraordinary!" murmured Mr. Tredgold.

"I didn't know him," attested Mr. Stobell, continuing to regard Mr. Chalk with much interest.

"I can't make head or tail of it," complained Mr. Chalk. "What about the ladies?"

Captain Brisket shook his head dismally and pointed ashore, and Mr. Chalk, following the direction of his finger, gazed spellbound at a figure which was signalling wildly from the highest point. Tredgold and Stobell, approaching the side, waved their handkerchiefs in response.

"We must go back for them," said Mr. Chalk, firmly.

"What! in this wind, sir?" inquired Brisket, with an indulgent laugh. "You're too much of a sailor to think that's possible, I'm sure; and it's going to last."

"We must put up with the disappointment and do without'em," said Stobell.

Mr. Chalk gazed helplessly ashore. "But we've got their luggage," he cried.

"Duckett sent it ashore," said Brisket. "Thinking that there was men's work ahead, and that the ladies might be in the way, he put it over the side and sent it back. And mind, believing what he did, I'm not saying he wasn't in the right."

Mr. Chalk again professed his inability to make head or tail of the proceedings. Ultimately—due time having been given for Captain Brisket's invention to get under way—he learned that a dyspeptic seaman, mistaking the mate's back for that of the cook, had first knocked his cap over his eyes and then pushed him over. "And that, of course," concluded the captain, "couldn't be allowed anyway, but, seeing that it was a mistake, we let the chap off."

"There's one thing about it," said Tredgold, as Chalk was about to speak; "it's shown us the stuff you're made of, Chalk."

"He frightened me," said Brisket, solemnly. "I own it. When I saw him come up like that I lost my nerve."

Mr. Chalk cast a final glance at the dwindling figure on the cliff, and then went silently below and stood in a pleasant reverie before the smashed door. He came to the same conclusion regarding the desperate nature of his character as the others; and the nervous curiosity of the men, who took sly peeps at him, and the fact that the cook dropped the soup-tureen that evening when he turned and found Mr. Chalk at his elbow, only added to his satisfaction.

He felt less heroic next morning. The wind had freshened during the night, and the floor of the cabin heaved in a sickening fashion beneath his feet as he washed himself. The atmosphere was stifling; timbers creaked and strained, and boots and other articles rolled playfully about the floor.

The strong, sweet air above revived him, but the deck was wet and cheerless and the air chill. Land had disappeared, and a tumbling waste of grey seas and a leaden sky was all that met his gaze. Nevertheless, he spoke warmly of the view to Captain Brisket, rather than miss which he preferred to miss his breakfast, contenting himself with half a biscuit and a small cup of tea on deck. The smell of fried bacon and the clatter of cups and saucers came up from below.

The heavy clouds disappeared and the sun came out. The sea changed from grey to blue, and Tredgold and Stobell, coming on deck after a good breakfast, arranged a couple of chairs and sat down to admire the scene. Aloft the new sails shone white in the sun, and spars and rigging creaked musically. A little spray came flying at intervals over the bows as the schooner met the seas.

"Lovely morning, sir," said Captain Brisket, who had been for some time exchanging glances with Stobell and Tredgold; "so calm and peaceful."

"Bu'ful," said Mr. Chalk, shortly. He was gazing in much distaste at a brig to starboard, which was magically drawn up to the skies one moment and blotted from view the next.

"Nice fresh smell," said Tredgold, sniffing. "Have a cigar, Chalk?"

Mr. Chalk shook his head, and his friend, selecting one from his case, lit it with a fusee that poisoned the atmosphere.

"None of us seem to be sea-sick," he remarked.

"Sea-sickness, sir," said Captain Brisket—"seasickness is mostly imagination. People think they're going to be bad, and they are. But there's one certain cure for it."

"Cure?" said Mr. Chalk, turning a glazing eye upon him.

"Yes, sir," said Brisket, with a warning glance at Mr. Stobell, who was grinning broadly. "It's old-fashioned and I've heard it laughed at, but it's a regular good old remedy. Mr. Stobell's laughing at it," he continued, as a gasping noise from that gentleman called for explanation, "but it's true all the same."

"What is it?" inquired Mr. Chalk, with feeble impatience.

"Pork," replied Captain Brisket, with impressive earnestness. "All that anybody's got to do is to get a bit o' pork-fat pork, mind you—and get the cook to stick a fork into it and frizzle it, all bubbling and spluttering, over the galley fire. Better still, do it yourself; the smell o' the cooking being part of——"

Mr. Chalk arose and, keeping his legs with difficulty, steadied himself for a moment with his hands on the companion, and disappeared below.

"There's nothing like it," said Brisket, turning with a satisfied smile to Mr. Stobell, who was sitting with his hands on his knees and rumbling with suppressed mirth. "It's an odd thing, but, if a man's disposed to be queer, you've only got to talk about that to finish him. Why talking about fried bacon should be so bad for 'em I don't know."

"Imagination," said Tredgold, smoking away placidly.

Brisket smiled and then, nursing his knee, scowled fiercely at the helmsman, who was also on the broad grin.

"Of course, it wants proper telling," he continued, turning to Stobell. "Did you notice his eyes when I spoke of it bubbling and spluttering over the galley fire?"

"I did," replied Mr. Stobell, laying his pipe carefully on the deck.

"Some people tell you to tie the pork to a bit o' string after frying it," said Brisket, "but that's what I call overdoing it. I think it's quite enough to describe its cooking, don't you?"

"Plenty," said Stobell. "Have one o' my matches," he said, proffering his box to Tredgold, who was about to relight his cigar with a fusee.

"Thanks, I prefer this," said Tredgold.

Mr. Stobell put his box in his pocket again and, sitting lumpily in his chair, gazed in a brooding fashion at the side.

"Talking about pork," began Brisket, "reminds me—"

"What! ain't you got over that joke yet?" inquired Mr. Stobell, glaring at him. "Poor Chalk can't help his feelings."

"No, no," said the captain, staring back.

"People can't help being sea-sick," said Stobell, fiercely.

"Certainly not, sir," agreed the captain.

"There's no disgrace in it," continued Mr. Stobell, with unusual fluency, "and nothing funny about it that I can see."

"Certainly not, sir," said the perplexed captain again. "I was just going to point out to you how, talking about pork—"

"I know you was," stormed Mr. Stobell, rising from his chair and lurching forward heavily. "D'ye think I couldn't hear you? Prating, and prating, and pra——"

He disappeared below, and the captain, after exchanging a significant grin with Mr. Tredgold, put his hands behind his back and began to pace the deck, musing solemnly on the folly of trusting to appearances.

Sea-sickness wore off after a day or two, and was succeeded by the monotony of life on board a small ship. Week after week they saw nothing but sea and sky, and Mr. Chalk, thirsting for change, thought with wistful eagerness of the palm-girt islands of the Fijian Archipelago to which Captain Brisket had been bidden to steer. In the privacy of their own cabin the captain and Mr. Duckett discussed with great earnestness the nature of the secret which they felt certain was responsible for the voyage.

CHAPTER XVI

It is an article of belief with some old-fashioned people that children should have no secrets from their parents, and, though not a model father in every way, Mr. Vickers felt keenly the fact that his daughter was keeping something from him. On two or three occasions since the date of sailing of the *Fair Emily* she had relieved her mind by throwing out dark hints of future prosperity, and there was no doubt that, somewhere in the house, she had a hidden store of gold. With his left foot glued to the floor he had helped her look for a sovereign one day which had rolled from her purse, and twice she had taken her mother on expensive journeys to Tollminster.

Brooding over the lack of confidence displayed by Selina, he sat on the side of her bed one afternoon glancing thoughtfully round the room. He was alone in the house, and now, or never, was his opportunity. After an hour's arduous toil he had earned tenpence-halfpenny, and, rightly considering that the sum was unworthy of the risk, put it back where he had found it, and sat down gloomily to peruse a paper which he had found secreted at the bottom of her box.

Mr. Vickers was but a poor scholar, and the handwriting was deplorable. Undotted "i's" travelled incognito through the scrawl, and uncrossed "t's" passed themselves off unblushingly as "l's." After half an hour's steady work, his imagination excited by one or two words which he had managed to decipher, he abandoned the task in despair, and stood moodily looking out of the window. His gaze fell upon Mr. William Russell, standing on the curb nearly opposite, with his hands thrust deep in his trouser-pockets, and, after a slight hesitation, he pushed open the small casement and beckoned him in.

"You're a bit of a scholar, ain't you, Bill?" he inquired.

Mr. Russell said modestly that he had got the name for it.

Again Mr. Vickers hesitated, but he had no choice, and his curiosity would brook no delay. With a strong caution as to secrecy, he handed the paper over to his friend.

Mr. Russell, his brow corrugated with thought, began to read slowly to himself. The writing was certainly difficult, but the watching Mr. Vickers saw by the way his friend's finger moved along the lines that he was conquering it. By the slow but steady dilation of Mr. Russell's eyes and the gradual opening of his mouth, he also saw that the contents were occasioning him considerable surprise.

"What does it say?" he demanded, anxiously.

Mr. Russell paid no heed. He gave vent to a little gurgle of astonishment and went on. Then he stopped and looked up blankly.

"Well, I'm d—-d!" he said.

"What is it?" cried Mr. Vickers.

Mr. Russell read on, and such exclamations as "Well, I'm jiggered!" "Well, I'm blest!" and others of a more complicated nature continued to issue from his lips.

"What's it all about?" shouted the excited Mr. Vickers.

Mr. Russell looked up and blinked at him. "I can't believe it," he murmured. "It's like a fairy tale, ain't it? What do you think of it?"

The exasperated Mr. Vickers, thrusting him back in his chair, shouted insults in his ear until his friend, awaking to the true position of affairs, turned to the beginning again and proceeded with much unction to read aloud the document that Mr. Tredgold had given to Selina some months before. Mr. Vickers listened in a state of amazement which surpassed his friend's, and, the reading finished, besought him to go over it again. Mr. Russell complied, and having got to the end put the paper down and gazed enviously at his friend.

"You won't have to do no more work," he said, wistfully.

"Not if I 'ad my rights," said Mr. Vickers. "It's like a dream, ain't it?"

"They bought a ship, so I 'eard," murmured the other; "they've got eight or nine men aboard, and they'll be away pretty near a year. Why, Selina'll 'ave a fortune."

Mr. Vickers, sitting with his legs stretched out stiffly before him, tried to think. "A lot o' good it'll do me," he said, bitterly. "It's young Joseph Tasker that'll get the benefit of it."

Mr. Russell whistled. "I'd forgot him," he exclaimed, "but I expect she only took him becos she couldn't get anybody else."

Mr. Vickers eyed him sternly, but, reflecting that Selina was well able to fight her own battles, forbore to reply.

"She must ha' told him," pursued Mr. Russell, following up a train of thought. "Nobody in their senses would want to marry Selina for anything else."

"Ho! indeed," said Mr. Vickers, coldly.

"Unless they was mad," admitted the other. "What are you going to do about it?" he inquired, suddenly.

"I shall think it over," said Mr. Vickers, with dignity. "As soon as you've gone I shall sit down with a quiet pipe and see what's best to be done."

Mr. Russell nodded approval. "First thing you do, you put the paper back where you got it from," he said, warningly.

"I know what I'm about," said Mr. Vickers. "I shall think it over when you're gone and make up my mind what to do."

"Don't you do nothing in a hurry," advised Mr. Russell, earnestly. "I'm going to think it, over, too."

Mr. Vickers stared at him in surprise. "You?" he said, disagreeably.

"Yes, me," replied the other. "After all, what's looks? Looks ain't everything."

His friend looked bewildered, and then started furiously as the meaning of Mr. Russell's remark dawned upon him. He began to feel like a miser beset by thieves.

"What age do you reckon you are, Bill?" he inquired, after a long pause.

"I'm as old as I look," replied Mr. Russell, simply, "and I've got a young face. I'd sooner it was anybody else than Selina; but, still, you can't 'ave everything. If she don't take me sooner than young Joseph I shall be surprised."

Mr. Vickers regarded him with undisguised astonishment.

"I might ha' married scores o' times if I'd liked," said Mr. Russell, with a satisfied air.

"Don't you go doing nothing silly," said Mr. Vickers, uneasily. "Selina can't abear you. You drink too much. Why, she's talking about making young Joseph sign the pledge, to keep'im steady."

Mr. Russell waved his objections aside. "I can get round her," he said, with cheery confidence. "I ain't kept ferrets all these years for nothing. I'm not going to let all that money slip through my fingers for want of a little trying."

He began his courtship a few days afterwards in a fashion which rendered Mr. Vickers almost helpless with indignation. In full view of Selina, who happened to be standing by the door, he brought her unfortunate father along Mint Street, holding him by the arm and addressing him in fond but severe tones on the surpassing merits of total abstinence and the folly of wasting his children's money on beer.

"I found 'im inside the 'Horse and Groom,'" he said to the astonished Selina; "they've got a new barmaid there, and the pore gal wasn't in the house 'arf an hour afore she was serving him with beer. A pot, mind you."

He shook his head in great regret at the speechless Mr. Vickers, and, pushing him inside the house, followed close behind.

"Look here, Bill Russell, I don't want any of your larks," said Miss Vickers, recovering herself.

"Larks?" repeated Mr. Russell, with an injured air. "I'm a teetotaler, and it's my duty to look after brothers that go astray."

He produced a pledge-card from his waistcoat-pocket and, smoothing it out on the table, pointed with great pride to his signature. The date of the document lay under the ban of his little finger.

"I'd just left the Temperance Hall," continued the zealot. "I've been to three meetings in two days; they'd been talking about the new barmaid, and I guessed at once what brother Vickers would do, an' I rushed off, just in the middle of brother Humphrey's experiences—and very interesting they was, too—to save him. He was just starting his second pot, and singing in between, when I rushed in and took the beer away from him and threw it on the floor."

"I wasn't singing," snarled Mr. Vickers, endeavouring to avoid his daughter's eye.

"Oh, my dear friend!" said Mr. Russell, who had made extraordinary progress in temperance rhetoric in a very limited time, "that's what comes o' the drink; it steals away your memory."

Miss Vickers trembled with wrath. "How dare you go into public-houses after I told you not to?" she demanded, stamping her foot.

"We must 'ave patience," said Mr. Russell, gently. "We must show the backslider 'ow much happier he would be without it. I'll 'elp you watch him."

"When I want your assistance I'll ask you for it," said Miss Vickers, tartly. "What do you mean by shoving your nose into other people's affairs?"

"It's—it's my duty to look after fallen brothers," said Mr. Russell, somewhat taken aback.

"What d'ye mean by fallen?" snapped Miss Vickers, confronting him fiercely.

"Fallen into a pub," explained Mr. Russell, hastily; "anybody might fall through them swing-doors; they're made like that o' purpose."

"You've fell through a good many in your time," interposed Mr. Vickers, with great bitterness.

"I know I 'ave," said the other, sadly; "but never no more. Oh, my friend, if you only knew how 'appy I feel since I've give up the drink! If you only knew what it was to 'ave your own self-respeck! Think of standing up on the platform and giving of your experiences! But I don't despair, brother; I'll have you afore I've done with you."

Mr. Vickers, unable to contain himself, got up and walked about the room. Mr. Russell, with a smile charged with brotherly love, drew a blank pledge-card from his pocket and, detaining him as he passed, besought him to sign it.

"He'll do it in time," he said in a loud whisper to Selina, as his victim broke loose. "I'll come in of an evening and talk to him till he does sign."

Miss Vickers hesitated, but, observing the striking improvement in the visitor's attire effected by temperance, allowed a curt refusal to remain unspoken. Mr. Vickers protested hotly.

"That'll do," said his daughter, indecision vanishing at sight of her father's opposition; "if Bill Russell likes to come in and try and do you good, he can."

Mr. Vickers said that he wouldn't have him, but under compulsion stayed indoors the following evening, while Mr. Russell, by means of coloured diagrams, cheerfully lent by his new friends, tried to show him the inroads made by drink upon the human frame. He sat, as Miss Vickers remarked, like a wooden image, and was only moved to animation by a picture of cirrhosis of the liver, which he described as being very pretty.

At the end of a week Mr. Vickers's principles remained unshaken, and so far Mr. Russell had made not the slightest progress in his designs upon the affections of Selina. That lady, indeed, treated him with but scant courtesy, and on two occasions had left him to visit Mr. Tasker; Mr. Vickers's undisguised amusement at such times being hard to bear.

"Don't give up, Bill," he said, encouragingly, as Mr. Russell sat glum and silent; "read over them beautiful 'Verses to a Tea-pot' agin, and try and read them as if you 'adn't got your mouth full o' fish-bait. You're wasting time."

"I don't want none o' your talk," said his disappointed friend. "If you ain't careful I'll tell Selina about you going up to her papers."

The smile faded from Mr. Vickers's face. "Don't make mischief, Bill," he said, uneasily.

"Well, don't you try and make fun o' me," said Mr. Russell, ferociously. "Taking the pledge is 'ard enough to bear without having remarks from you."

"I didn't mean them to be remarks, Bill," said the other, mildly. "But if you tell about me, you know, Selina'll see through your little game."

"I'm about sick o' the whole thing," said Mr. Russell, desperately. "I ain't 'ad a drink outside o' my own house for pretty near a fortnight. I shall ask Selina to-morrow night, and settle it."

"Ask her?" said the amazed Mr. Vickers. "Ask 'er what?"

"Ask 'er to marry me," said the other, doggedly.

Mr. Vickers, thoroughly alarmed, argued with him in vain, the utmost concession he could wring from the determined Mr. Russell being a promise to give him a hint to get out of the way.

"I'll do that for my own sake," he said, frankly. "I can do it better alone, and if your old woman is in you get her out too. Ask 'er to go for a walk; that'll please Selina. I don't know what the gal does want. I thought turning teetotaler and setting a good example to you would do the trick, if anything would."

Mrs. Vickers's utter astonishment next evening, when her husband asked her to go for a walk, irritated that gentleman almost beyond endurance. Convinced at last that he was not joking, she went upstairs and put on her bonnet, and then stood waiting for the reluctant Mr. Vickers with an air of almost bashful diffidence.

"Joseph is coming in soon," said Selina, as her parents moved to the door. "I'm expecting him every minute."

"I'll stop and see 'im," said Mr. Russell. "There's something I want to speak to him about partikler."

Mr. Vickers gave a warning glance at him as he went out, and trembled as he noted his determined aspect. In a state of considerable agitation he took hold of his wife by the elbow and propelled her along.

It was a cold night, and a strong easterly wind had driven nearly everybody else indoors. Mr. Vickers shivered, and, moving at a good pace, muttered something to his astonished wife about "a good country walk." They quitted the streets and plunged into dark lanes until, in Mr. Vickers's judgment, sufficient time having elapsed for the worst to have happened, they turned and made their way to the town again.

"There's somebody outside our house," said Mrs. Vickers, who had been in a state of amazed discomfort the whole time.

Mr. Vickers approached warily. Two people were on the doorstep in the attitude of listeners, while a third was making strenuous attempts to peep through at the side of the window-blind. From inside came the sound of voices raised in dispute, that of Selina's being easily distinguishable.

"What—what's all this?" demanded Mr. Vickers, in trembling tones, as he followed his wife inside and closed the door.

He glanced from Selina, who was standing in front of Mr. Tasker in the manner of a small hen defending an overgrown chicken, to Mr. Russell, who was towering above them and trying to reach him.

"What's all this?" he repeated, with an attempt at pomposity.

The disputants all spoke at once: Mr. Russell with an air of jocular ferocity, Miss Vickers in a voice that trembled with passion, and Mr. Tasker speaking as a man with a grievance. Despite the confusion, Mr. Vickers soon learned that it was a case of "two's company and three's none," and that Mr. Russell, after turning a deaf ear to hints to retire which had gradually increased in bluntness, had suddenly turned restive and called Mr. Tasker a "mouldy image," a "wall-eyed rabbit," and divers other obscure and contradictory things. Not content with that, he had, without any warning, kissed Miss Vickers, and when Mr. Tasker, obeying that infuriated damsel's commands, tried to show him the door, had facetiously offered to show that gentleman the wall and taken him up, and bumped him against it until they were both tired.

"Anybody would ha' thought I was hurting 'im by the noise he made," said the impenitent Mr. Russell.

"I—I'm surprised at you, Bill," said Mr. Vickers, nervously.

"Put him outside," cried Selina, stamping her foot.

"You'd better get off 'ome, Bill," said Mr. Vickers, with a persuasive wink.

"While you're safe," added his daughter, with a threatening gesture.

"Go and get yourself 'arf a pint o' warm lemonade," chimed in the voice of the daring Joseph.

Mr. Russell stepped towards him, but Mr. Vickers, seizing him by the coat, held him back and implored him to remember where he was.

"I'd bump the lot of you for two pins," said the disappointed Mr. Russell, longingly. "And it'ud do you good; you'd all be the better for it. You'd know 'ow to behave to people when they come in to see you, then. As for Selina, I wouldn't marry her now for all her money."

"Money?" said the irate Selina, scornfully. "What money?"

"The money in the paper," said Mr. Russell, with a diabolical leer in the direction of the unfortunate Mr. Vickers. "The paper what your father found in your box. Didn't he tell you?"

He kicked over a chair which stood in his way and, with a reckless swagger, strode to the door. At the "Horse and Groom," where he spent the remainder of the evening, he was so original in his remarks upon women that two unmarried men offered to fight him, and were only appeased by hearing a full and true account of the circumstances responsible for so much bitterness.

CHAPTER XVII

"TRIED!" said Captain Bowers, indignantly. "I have tried, over and over again, but it's no use."

"Have you tried the right way?" suggested Ed ward Tredgold.

"I've tried every way," replied Captain Bowers, impatiently.

"We must think of another, then," said the imperturbable Edward. "Have some more beef?" The captain passed his plate up. "You should have seen her when I said that I was coming to supper with you this evening," he said, impressively. Mr. Tredgold laid down the carving knife and fork. "What did she say?" he inquired, eagerly. "Grunted," said the captain. "Nonsense," said the other, sharply.

"I tell you she did," retorted the captain. "She didn't say a word; just grunted."

"I know what you mean," said Mr. Tredgold; "only you are not using the right word."

"All right," said the captain, resignedly; "I don't know a grunt when I hear it, then; that's all. She generally does grunt if I happen to mention your name."

Mr. Tredgold resumed his meal and sat eating in silence. The captain, who was waiting for more beef, became restless.

"I hope my plate isn't in your way," he said, at last.

"Not at all," said the other, absently.

"Perhaps you'll pass it back to me, then," said the captain.

Mr. Tredgold, still deep in thought, complied. "I wish I could persuade you to have a little more," he said, in tones of polite regret. "I've often noticed that big men are small eaters. I wonder why it is?"

"Sometimes it is because they can't get it, I expect," said the indignant captain.

Mr. Tredgold said that no doubt that was the case sometimes, and was only recalled to the true position of affairs by the hungry captain marching up to the beef and carving for himself.

"I'm sorry," he said, with a laugh. "I was thinking of something else. I wonder whether you would let me use the crow's-nest for a day or two? There's a place we have got on our hands, a mile or two out, and I want to keep my eye on it."

The captain, his good humour quite restored, preserved his gravity with an effort. "I don't see that she could object to that," he said, slowly. "It's a matter of business, as you might say."

"Of course, I could go straight round to the back without troubling you," resumed Mr. Tredgold. "It's so awkward not to be able to see you when I want to."

Captain Bowers ventured a sympathetic wink. "It's awkward not to be able to see anybody when you want to," he said, softly.

Two days later Miss Drewitt, peeping cautiously from her bedroom window, saw Mr. Tredgold perched up in the crow's-nest with the telescope. It was a cold, frosty day in January, and she smiled agreeably as she hurried downstairs to the fire and tried to imagine the temperature up aloft.

Stern in his attention to duty, Mr. Tredgold climbed day after day to his post of observation and kept a bored but whimsical eye on a deserted cowhouse three miles off. On the fourth day the captain was out, and Miss Drewitt, after a casual peep from the kitchen window, shrugged her shoulders and returned to the sitting-room.

"Mr. Tredgold must be very cold up there, Miss," said Mr. Tasker, respectfully, as he brought in the tea. "He keeps slapping his chest and blowing on his fingers to keep 'imself warm."

Miss Drewitt said "Oh!" and, drawing the little table up to her easy-chair, put down her book and poured herself out a cup of tea. She had just arranged it to her taste-two lumps of sugar and a liberal allowance of cream—when a faint rap sounded on the front door.

"Come in!" she said, taking her feet from the fender and facing about.

The door opened and revealed to her indignant gaze the figure of Mr. Tredgold. His ears and nose were of a brilliant red and his eyes were watering with the cold. She eyed him inquiringly.

"Good afternoon," he said, bowing.

Miss Drewitt returned the greeting.

"Isn't Captain Bowers in?" said Mr. Tredgold, with a shade of disappointment in his voice as he glanced around.

"No," said the girl.

Mr. Tredgold hesitated. "I was going to ask him to give me a cup of tea," he said, with a shiver. "I'm half frozen, and I'm afraid that I have a taken a chill."

Miss Drewitt nearly dropped her tea-cup in surprise at his audacity. He was certainly very cold, and she noticed a little blue mixed with the red of his nose. She looked round the cosy room and then at the open door, which was causing a bitter draught.

"He is not in," she repeated.

"Thank you," said Mr. Tredgold, patiently. "Good afternoon."

He was so humble that the girl began to feel uncomfortable. His gratitude for nothing reminded her of a disappointed tramp; moreover, the draught from the door was abominable.

"I can give you a cup of tea, if you wish," she said, shivering. "But please make haste and shut that door."

Mr. Tredgold stepped inside and closed it with alacrity, his back being turned just long enough to permit a congratulatory wink at the unconscious oak. He took a chair the other side of the fire, and, extending his numbed fingers to the blaze, thanked her warmly.

"It is very kind of you," he said, as he took his cup from her. "I was half frozen."

"I should have thought that a brisk walk home would have been better for you," said the girl, coldly.

Mr. Tredgold shook his head dolefully. "I should probably only have had lukewarm tea when I got there," he replied. "Nobody looks after me properly."

He passed his cup up and began to talk of skating and other seasonable topics. As he got warmer and his features regained their normal colouring and his face its usual expression of cheerfulness, Miss Drewitt's pity began to evaporate.

"Are you feeling better?" she inquired, pointedly.

"A little," was the cautious reply. His face took on an expression of anxiety and he spoke of a twinge, lightly tapping his left lung by way of emphasis.

"I hope that I shall not be taken ill here," he said, gravely.

Miss Drewitt sat up with a start. "I should hope not," she said, sharply.

"So inconvenient," he murmured.

"Quite impossible," said Miss Drewitt, whose experience led her to believe him capable of anything.

"I should never forgive myself," he said, gently.

Miss Drewitt regarded him in alarm, and of her own accord gave him a third cup of tea and told him that he might smoke. She felt safer when she saw him light a cigarette, and, for fear that a worse thing might befall her, entered amiably into conversation. She even found herself, somewhat to her surprise, discussing the voyage and sympathising with Mr. Tredgold in his anxiety concerning his father's safety.

"Mrs. Chalk and Mrs. Stobell are very anxious, too," he said. "It is a long way for a small craft like that."

"And then to find no treasure at the end of it," said Miss Drewitt, with feminine sweetness.

Mr. Tredgold stole a look at her. "I did not mean to say that the captain had no treasure," he said, quietly.

"You believe in it now?" said the girl, triumphantly.

"I believe that the captain has a treasure," admitted the other, "certainly."

"Worth half a million?" persisted Miss Drewitt.

"Worth more than that," said Mr. Tredgold, gazing steadily into the fire.

The girl looked puzzled. "More?" she said, in surprise.

"Much more," said the other, still contemplating the fire. "It is priceless."

Miss Drewitt sat up suddenly and then let herself back slowly into the depths of the chair. Her face turned scarlet and she hoped fervently that if Mr. Tredgold looked at her the earth might open and swallow him up. She began to realize dimly that in the absence of an obliging miracle of that kind there would never be any getting rid of him.

"Priceless," repeated Mr. Tredgold, in challenging tones.

Miss Drewitt made no reply. Rejoinder was dangerous and silence difficult. In a state of nervous indignation she rang for Mr. Tasker and instructed him to take away the tea-things; to sweep the hearth; and to alter the position of two pictures. By the time all this was accomplished she had regained her wonted calm and was airing some rather strong views on the subject of two little boys who lived with a catapult next door but one.

CHAPTER XVIII

Month by month the *Fair Emily* crept down south. The Great Bear and other constellations gave way to the stars of the southern skies, and Mr. Chalk tried hard not to feel disappointed with the arrangement of those in the Southern Cross. Pressed by the triumphant Brisket, to whom he voiced his views, he had to admit that it was at least as much like a cross as the other was a bear.

As they got farther south he had doffed his jersey and sea boots in favour of a drill suit and bare feet. In this costume, surmounted by a Panama hat, he was the only thing aboard that afforded the slightest amusement to Mr. Stobell, whose temper was suffering severely under a long spell of monotonous idleness, and whose remarks concerning the sea and everything in connection with it were so strangely out of keeping with the idea of a pleasure cruise that Mr. Tredgold lectured him severely on his indiscretion.

"Stobell is no more doing this for pleasure than I am," said Captain Brisket to Mr. Duckett. "It's something big that's brought him all this way, you mark my words."

The mate nodded acquiescence. "What about Mr. Chalk?" he said, in a low voice. "Can't you get it out of him?"

"Shuts up like an oyster directly I get anywhere near it," replied the captain; "sticks to it that it is a yachting trip and that Tredgold is studying the formations of islands. Says he has got a list of them he is going to visit."

"Mr. Tredgold was talking the same way to me," said the mate. "He says he's going to write a book about them when he goes back. He asked me what I thought'ud be a good title."

"I know what would be a good title for him," growled Brisket, as Mr. Stobell came on deck and gazed despondently over the side. "We're getting towards the end of our journey, sir."

"End?" said Mr. Stobell. "End? I don't believe there is an end. I believe you've lost your way and we shall go sailing on and on for ever."

He walked aft and, placing himself in a deckchair, gazed listlessly at the stolid figure of the helmsman. The heat was intense, and both Tredgold and Chalk had declined to proceed with a conversation limited almost entirely on his side to personal abuse. He tried the helmsman, and made that unfortunate thirsty for a week by discussing the rival merits of bitter ale in a pewter and stout in a china mug. The helmsman, a man of liberal ideas, said, with some emotion, that he could drink either of them out of a flower-pot.

Mr. Chalk became strangely restless as they neared their goal. He had come thousands of miles and had seen nothing fresh with the exception of a few flying-fish, an albatross, and a whale blowing in the distance. Pacing the deck late one night with Captain Brisket he expressed mild yearnings for a little excitement.

"You want adventure," said the captain, shaking his head at him. "I know you. Ah, what a sailorman you'd ha' made. With a crew o' six like yourself I'd take this little craft anywhere. The way you pick up seamanship is astonishing. Peter Duckett swears you must ha' been at sea as a boy, and all I can do I can't persuade him otherwise."

"I always had a feeling that I should like it," said Mr. Chalk, modestly.

"Like it!" repeated the captain. "O' course you do; you've got the salt in your blood, but this peaceful cruising is beginning to tell on you. There's a touch o' wildness in you, sir, that's always struggling to come to the front. Peter Duckett was saying the same thing only the other day. He's very uneasy about it."

"Uneasy!" repeated Mr. Chalk.

"Aye," said the captain, drawing a deep breath. "And if I tell you that I am too, it wouldn't be outside the truth."

"But why?" inquired Mr. Chalk, after they had paced once up and down the deck in silence.

"It's the mystery we don't like," said Brisket, at last. "How are we to know what desperate venture you are going to let us in for? Follow you faithful we will, but we don't like going in the dark; it ain't quite fair to us."

"There's not the slightest danger in the world," said Mr. Chalk, with impressive earnestness.

"But there's a mystery; you can't deny that," said the captain.

Mr. Chalk cleared his throat. "It's a secret," he said, slowly.

"From me?" inquired the captain, in reproachful accents.

"It isn't my secret," said Mr. Chalk. "So far as I'm concerned I'd tell you with pleasure."

The captain slowly withdrew his arm from Mr. Chalk's, and moving to the side leaned over it with his shoulders hunched. Somewhat moved by this display of feeling, Mr. Chalk for some time hesitated to disturb him, and when at last he did steal up and lay a friendly hand on the captain's shoulder it was gently shaken off.

"Secrets!" said Brisket, in a hollow voice. "From me! I ain't to be trusted?"

"It isn't my doing," said Mr. Chalk.

"Well, well, it don't matter, sir," said the captain. "Bill Brisket must put up with it. It's the first time in his life he's been suspected, and it's doubly hard coming from you. You've hurt me, sir, and there's no other man living could do that."

Mr. Chalk stood by in sorrowful perplexity.

"And I put my life in your hands," continued the captain, with a low, hard laugh. "You're the, only man in the world that knows who killed Smiling Peter in San Francisco, and I told you. Well, well!"

"But you did it in self-defence," said the other, eagerly.

"What does that matter?" said the captain, turning and walking forward, followed by the anxious Mr. Chalk. "I've got no proof of it. Open your mouth—once—and I swing for it. That's the extent of my trust in you."

Mr. Chalk, much affected, swore a few sailorly oaths as to what he wished might happen to him if he ever betrayed the other's confidence.

"Yes," said the captain, mournfully, "that's all very well; but you can't trust me in a smaller matter, however much I swear to keep it secret. And it's weighing on me in another way: I believe the crew have got an inkling of something, and here am I, master of the ship, responsible for all your lives, kept in ignorance."

"The crew!" ejaculated the startled Mr. Chalk.

Captain Brisket hesitated and lowered his voice. "The other night I came on deck for a look round and saw one of them peeping down through your skylight," he said, slowly. "I sent him below, and after he'd gone I looked down and saw you and Mr. Tredgold and Stobell all bending over a paper."

Mr. Chalk, deep in thought, paced up and down in silence.

"That's a secret," said Brisket. "I don't want them to think that I was spying. I told you because you understand. A shipmaster has to keep his eyes open, for everybody's sake."

"It's your duty," said Mr. Chalk, firmly.

Captain Brisket, with a little display of emotion, thanked him, and, leaning against the side, drew his attention to the beauty of the stars and sea. Impelled by the occasion and the charm of the night he waxed sentimental, and with a strange mixture of bluffness and shyness spoke of his aged mother, of the loneliness of a seafarer's life, and the inestimable boon of real friendship. He bared his inmost soul to his sympathetic listener, and then, affecting to think from a remark of Mr. Chalk's that he was going to relate the secret of the voyage, declined to hear it on the ground that he was only a rough sailorman and not to be trusted. Mr. Chalk, contesting this hotly, convinced him at last that he was in error, and then found that, bewildered by the argument, the captain had consented to be informed of a secret which he had not intended to impart.

"But, mind," said Brisket, holding up a warning finger, "I'm not going to tell Peter Duckett. There's no need for him to know."

Mr. Chalk said "Certainly not," and, seeing no way for escape, led the reluctant man as far from the helmsman as possible and whispered the information. By the time they parted for the night Captain Brisket knew as much as the members of the expedition themselves, and, with a rare thoughtfulness, quieted Mr. Chalk's conscience by telling him that he had practically guessed the whole affair from the beginning.

He listened with great interest a few days later when Mr. Tredgold, after considering audibly which island he should visit first, gave him the position of Bowers's Island and began to discuss coral reefs and volcanic action. They were now well in among the islands. Two they passed at a distance, and went so close to a third—a mere reef with a few palms upon it—that Mr. Chalk, after a lengthy inspection through his binoculars, was able to declare it uninhabited.

A fourth came into sight a couple of days later: a small grey bank on the starboard bow. Captain Brisket, who had been regarding it for some time with great care, closed his glass with a bang and stepped up to Mr. Tredgold.

"There she is, sir," he said, in satisfied tones.

Mr. Tredgold, who was drinking tea, put down his cup, and rose with an appearance of mild interest. Mr. Stobell followed suit, and both gazed in strong indignation at the undisguised excitement of Mr. Chalk as he raced up the rigging for a better view. Tredgold with the captain's glass, and Stobell with an old pair of field-glasses in which he had great faith, gazed from the deck. Tredgold was the first to speak.

"Are you sure this is the one, Brisket?" he inquired, carelessly.

"Certainly, sir," said the captain, in some surprise. "At least, it's the one you told me to steer for."

"Don't look much like the map," said Stobell, in a low aside. "Where's the mountain?"

Tredgold looked again. "I fancy it's a bit higher towards the middle," he said, after a prolonged inspection; "and, besides, it's 'mount,' not 'mountain.'"

Captain Brisket, who had with great delicacy drawn a little apart in recognition of their whispers, stepped towards them again.

"I don't know that I've ever seen this particular island before," he said, frankly; "likely not; but it's the one you told me to find. There's over a couple of hundred of them, large and small, knocking about. If you think you've made a mistake we might try some of the others."

"No," said Tredgold, after a pause and a prolonged inspection; "this must be right."

Mr. Chalk came down from aloft, his eyes shining with pure joy, and joined them.

"How long before we're alongside?" he inquired.

"Two hours," replied the captain; "perhaps three," he added, considering.

Mr. Chalk glanced aloft and, after a knowing question or two as to the wind, began in a low voice to converse with his friends. Mr. Tredgold's misgivings as to the identity of the island he dismissed at once as baseless. The mount satisfied him, and when, as they approached nearer, discrepancies in shape between the island and the map were pointed out to him he easily explained them by speaking of the difficulties of cartography to an amateur.

"There's our point," he said, indicating it with a forefinger, which the incensed Stobell at once struck down. "We couldn't have managed it better so far as time is concerned. We'll sleep ashore tonight in the tent and start the search at daybreak."

Captain Brisket approached the island cautiously. To the eyes of the voyagers it seemed to change shape as they neared it, until finally, the *Fair Emily* anchoring off the reef which guarded it, it revealed itself as a small island about three-quarters of a mile long and two or three hundred yards wide. A beach of coral sand shelved steeply to the sea, and a background of cocoa-nut trees and other vegetation completed a picture on which Mr. Chalk gazed with the rapture of a devotee at a shrine.

He went below as the anchor ran out, and after a short absence reappeared on deck bedizened with weapons. A small tent, with blankets and provisions, and a long deal box containing a couple of spades and a pick, were put into one of the boats, and the three friends, after giving minute instructions to the captain, followed. Mr. Duckett took the helm, and after a short pull along the edge of the reef discovered an opening which gave access to the smooth water inside.

"A pretty spot, gentlemen," he said, scanning the island closely. "I don't think that there is anybody on it."

"We'll go over it first and make sure," said Stobell, as the boat's nose ran into the beach. "Come along, Chalk."

He sprang out and, taking one of the guns, led the way along the beach, followed by Mr. Chalk. The men looked after them longingly, and then, in obedience to the mate, took the stores out of the boat and pitched the tent. By the time Chalk and Stobell returned they were seated in the boat and ready to depart.

A feeling of loneliness came over Mr. Chalk as he watched the receding boat. The schooner, riding at anchor half a mile outside the reef, had taken in her sails and presented a singularly naked and desolate appearance. He wondered how long it would take the devoted Brisket to send assistance in case of need, and blamed himself severely for not having brought some rockets for signalling purposes. Long before night came the prospect of sleeping ashore had lost all its charm.

"One of us ought to keep watch," he said, as Stobell, after a heavy supper followed by a satisfying pipe, rolled himself in a blanket and composed himself for slumber.

Mr. Stobell grunted, and in a few minutes was fast asleep. Mr. Tredgold, first blowing out the candle, followed suit, while Mr. Chalk, a prey to vague fears, sat up nursing a huge revolver.

The novelty of the position, the melancholy beat of the surge on the farther beach, and faint, uncertain noises all around kept him awake. He fancied that he heard stealthy footsteps on the beach, and low, guttural voices calling among the palms. Twice he aroused his friends and twice they sat up and reviled him.

"If you put your bony finger into my ribs again," growled Mr. Stobell, tenderly rubbing the afflicted part, "you and me won't talk alike. Like a bar of iron it was."

"I thought I heard something," said Mr. Chalk. "I should have fired, only I was afraid of scaring you."

"*Fired?*" repeated Mr. Stobell, thoughtfully. "*Fired?* Was it the barrel of that infernal pistol you shoved into my ribs just now?"

"I just touched you with it," admitted the other. "I'm sorry if I hurt you."

Mr. Stobell, feeling in his pocket, struck a match and held it up. "Full cock," he said, in a broken voice; "and he stirred me up with it. And then *he* talks of savages!"

He struck another match and lit the candle, and then, before Mr. Chalk could guess his intentions, pressed him backwards and took the pistol away. He raised the canvas and threw it out into the night, and then, remembering the guns, threw them after it. This done he blew out the candle, and in two minutes was fast asleep again.

An hour passed and Mr. Chalk, despite his fears, began to nod. Half asleep, he lay down and drew his blanket about him, and then he sat up suddenly wide awake as an unmistakable footstep sounded outside.

For a few seconds he sat unable to move; then he stretched out his hand and began to shake Stobell. He could have sworn that hands were fumbling at the tent.

"Eh?" said Stobell, sleepily.

Chalk shook him again. Stobell sat up angrily, but before he could speak a wild yell rent the air, the tent collapsed suddenly, and they struggled half suffocated in the folds of the canvas.

CHAPTER XIX

Mr. Stobell was the first to emerge, and, seizing the canvas, dragged it free of the writhing bodies of his companions. Mr. Chalk gained his feet and, catching sight of some dim figures standing a few yards away on the beach, gave a frantic shout and plunged into the interior, followed by the others. A shower of pieces of coral whizzing by their heads and another terrible yell accelerated their flight.

Mr. Chalk gained the farther beach unmolested and, half crazy with fear, ran along blindly. Footsteps, which he hoped were those of his friends, pounded away behind him, and presently Stobell, panting heavily, called to him to stop. Mr. Chalk, looking over his shoulder, slackened his pace and allowed him to overtake him.

"Wait—for—Tredgold," said Stobell, breathlessly, as he laid a heavy hand on his shoulder.

Mr. Chalk struggled to free himself. "Where is he?" He gasped.

Stobell, still holding him, stood trying to regain his breath. "They— they must—have got him," he said, at last. "Have you got any of your pistols on you?"

"You threw them all away," quavered Mr. Chalk. "I've only got a knife."

He fumbled with trembling fingers at his belt; Stobell brushing his hand aside drew a sailor's knife from its sheath, and started to run back in the direction of the tent. Mr. Chalk, after a moment's hesitation, followed a little way behind.

"Look out!" he screamed, and stopped suddenly, as a figure burst out of the trees on to the beach a score of yards ahead. Stobell, with a hoarse cry, raised his hand and dashed at it.

"Stobell!" cried a voice.

"It's Tredgold," cried Stobell. He waited for him to reach them, and then, turning, all three ran stumbling along the beach.

They ran in silence until they reached the other end of the island. So far there were no signs of pursuit, and Stobell, breathing hard from his unwonted exercise, collected a few lumps of coral and piled them on the beach.

"They had me over—twice," said Tredgold, jerkily; "they tore the clothes from my back. How I got away I don't know. I fought—kicked—then suddenly I broke loose and ran."

He threw himself on the beach and drew his breath in long, sobbing gasps. Stobell, going a few paces forward, peered into the darkness and listened intently.

"I suppose they're waiting for daylight," he said at last.

He sat down on the beach and, after making a few disparaging remarks about coral as a weapon, lapsed into silence.

To Mr. Chalk it seemed as though the night would never end. A dozen times he sprang to his feet and gazed fearfully into the darkness, and a dozen times at least he reminded the silent Stobell of the folly of throwing other people's guns away. Day broke at last and showed him Tredgold in a tattered shirt and a pair of trousers, and Stobell sitting close by sound asleep.

"We must try and signal to the ship," he said, in a hoarse whisper. "It's our only chance."

Tredgold nodded assent and shook Stobell quietly. The silence was oppressive. They rose and peered out to sea, and a loud exclamation broke from all three. The "*Fair Emily*" had disappeared.

Stobell rubbed his eyes and swore softly; Tredgold and Chalk stood gazing in blank dismay at the unbroken expanse of shining sea.

"The savages must have surprised them," said the latter, in trembling tones. "That's why they left us alone."

"Or else they heard the noise ashore and put to sea," said Tredgold.

They stood gazing at each other in consternation. Then Stobell, who had been looking about him, gave vent to an astonished grunt and pointed to a boat drawn upon the beach nearly abreast of where their tent had been.

"Some of the crew have escaped ashore," said Mr. Chalk.

Striking inland, so as to get the shelter of the trees, they made their way cautiously towards the boat. Colour was lent to Mr. Chalk's surmise by the fact that it was fairly well laden with stores. As they got near they saw a couple of small casks which he thought contained water, an untidy pile of tinned provisions, and two or three bags of biscuit. The closest search failed to reveal any signs of men, and plucking up courage they walked boldly down to the boat and stood gazing stupidly at its contents.

The firearms which Stobell had pitched out of the tent the night before lay in the bottom, together with boxes of cartridges from the cabin, a couple of axes, and a pile of clothing, from the top of which Mr. Tredgold, with a sharp exclamation, snatched a somewhat torn coat and waistcoat. From the former he drew out a bulky pocketbook, and, opening it with trembling fingers, hastily inspected the contents.

"The map has gone!" he shouted.

The others stared at him.

"Brisket has gone off with the ship," he continued, with desperate calmness. "It was the crew of our own schooner that frightened us off last night."

Mr. Stobell, still staring in a stony fashion, nodded slowly; Mr. Chalk after an effort found his voice.

"They've gone off with the treasure," he said, slowly.

"Also," continued Tredgold, "this is not Bowers's Island. I can see it all now. They've only taken the map, and now they're off to the real island to get the treasure. It's as clear as daylight."

"Broad daylight," said Stobell, huskily. "But how did they know?"

"Somebody has been talking," said Tredgold, in a hard voice. "Somebody has been confiding in that honest, open-hearted sailor, Captain Brisket."

He turned as he spoke and gazed fixedly at the open-mouthed Chalk. In a slower fashion, but with no less venom, Mr. Stobell also bent his regards upon that amiable but erring man.

Mr. Chalk returned their gaze with something like defiance. Half an hour before he had expected to have been killed and eaten. He had passed a night of horror, expecting death every minute. Now he exulted in the blue sky, the line of white breakers crashing on the reef, and the sea sparkling in the sunshine; and he had not spent twenty-five years with Mrs. Chalk without acquiring some skill in the noble art of self-defence.

"Ah, Brisket was trying to pump me a week ago," he said, confidentially. "I see it all now."

The others glared at him luridly.

"He said that he had seen us through the skylight studying a paper," continued Mr. Chalk, shaking his head. "I thought at the time you were rather rash, Tredgold."

Mr. Tredgold choked and, meeting the fault-finding eye of Mr. Stobell, began to protest.

"The thing Brisket couldn't understand," said Chalk, gaining confidence as he proceeded, "was Stobell's behaviour. He said that he couldn't believe that a man who grumbled at the sea so much as he did could be sailing for pleasure."

Mr. Stobell glowered fiercely. "Why didn't you tell us before?" he demanded.

"I didn't attach any importance to it," said Mr. Chalk, truthfully. "I thought that it was just curiosity on Brisket's part. It surprised me that he had been observing you and Tredgold so closely; that was all."

"Pity you didn't tell us," exclaimed Tredgold, harshly. "We might have been prepared, then."

"You ought to have told us at once," said Stobell.

Mr. Chalk agreed. "I ought to have done so, perhaps," he said, slowly; "only I was afraid of hurting your feelings. As it is, we must make the best of it. It is no good grumbling at each other."

"If I had had the map instead of Tredgold, perhaps this wouldn't have happened."

"It was a crazy idea to keep it in your coat-pocket," said Stobell, scowling at Tredgold. "No doubt Brisket saw you put it back there the other night, guessed what it was, and laid his plans according."

"If it hadn't been for your grumbling it wouldn't have happened," retorted Tredgold, hotly. "That's what roused his suspicions in the first instance."

Mr. Chalk interposed. "It is no good you two quarrelling about it," he said, with kindly severity. "The mischief is done. Bear a hand with these stores, and then help me to fix the tent up again."

The others hesitated, and then without a word Mr. Stobell worked one of the casks out of the boat and began to roll it up the beach. The tent still lay where it had fallen, but the case of spades had disappeared. They raised the tent again and carried in the stores, after which Mr. Chalk, with the air of an old campaigner, made a small fire and prepared breakfast.

Day by day they scanned the sea for any signs of a sail, but in vain. Cocoa-nuts and a few birds shot by Mr. Stobell—who had been an expert at pigeon-shooting in his youth—together with a species of fish which Mr. Chalk pronounced to be edible a few hours after the others had partaken of it, furnished them with a welcome change of diet. In the smooth water inside the reef they pulled about in the boat, and, becoming bolder and more expert in the management of it, sometimes ventured outside. Mr. Stobell pronounced the life to be more monotonous than that on board ship, and once, in a moment of severe depression, induced by five days' heavy rain, spoke affectionately of Mrs. Stobell. To Mr. Chalk's reminder that the rain had enabled them to replenish their water supply he made a churlish rejoinder.

He passed his time in devising plans for the capture and punishment of Captain Brisket, and caused a serious misunderstanding by expressing his regret that that unscrupulous mariner had not rendered himself liable to the extreme penalty of the law by knocking Mr. Chalk on the head on the night of the attack. His belated explanation that he wished Mr. Chalk no harm was pronounced by that gentleman to be childish.

"We can do nothing to Brisket even if we escape from this place," said Tredgold, peremptorily.

"Do nothing?" roared Stobell. "Why not?"

"In the first place we sha'n't find him," said Tredgold. "After they have got the treasure they will get rid of the ship and disperse all over the world."

Mr. Stobell, with heavy sarcasm, said that once, many years before, he had heard of people called detectives.

"In the second place," continued Tredgold, "we can't explain. It wasn't our map, and, strictly speaking, we had no business with it. Even if we caught Brisket, we should have no legal claim to the treasure. And if you want to blurt out to all Binchester how we were tricked and frightened out of our lives by imitation savages, I don't."

"He stole our ship," growled Stobell, after a long pause. "We could have him for that."

"Mutiny on the high seas," added Chalk, with an important air.

"The whole story would have to come out," said Tredgold, sharply. "Verdict: served them right. Once we had got the treasure we could have given Captain Bowers his share, or more than his share, and it would have been all right. As it is, nobody must know that we went for it."

Mr. Stobell, unable to trust himself with speech, stumped fiercely up and down the beach.

"But it will all have to come out if we are rescued," objected Mr. Chalk.

"We can tell what story we like," said Tredgold. "We can say that the schooner went to pieces on a reef in the night; we got separated from the other boat and made our way here. We have got plenty of time to concoct a story, and there is nobody to contradict it."

Mr. Stobell brought up in front of him and frowned thoughtfully. "I suppose you're right," he said, slowly; "but if we ever get off this chicken-perch, and I run across him, let him look out, that's all."

To pass the time they built themselves a hut on the beach in a situation where it would stand the best chance of being seen by any chance vessel. At one corner stood a mast fashioned from a tree, and a flag, composed for the most part of shirts which Mr. Chalk thought his friends had done with, fluttered bravely in the breeze. It was designed to attract attention, and, so far as the bereaved Mr. Stobell was concerned, it certainly succeeded.

CHAPTER XX

Nearly a year had elapsed since the sailing of the *Fair Emily*, and Binchester, which had listened doubtfully to the tale of the treasure as revealed by Mr. William Russell, was still awaiting news of her fate. Cablegrams to Sydney only elicited the information that she had not been heard of, and the opinion became general that she had added but one more to the many mysteries of the sea.

Captain Bowers, familiar with many cases of ships long overdue which had reached home in safety, still hoped, but it was clear from the way in which Mrs. Chalk spoke of her husband and the saint-like qualities she attributed to him that she never expected to see him again. Mr. Stobell also appeared to his wife through tear-dimmed eyes as a person of great gentleness and infinite self-sacrifice.

"All the years we were married," she said one afternoon to Mrs. Chalk, who had been listening with growing impatience to an account of Mr. Stobell which that gentleman would have been the first to disclaim, "I never gave him a cross word. Nothing was too good for me; I only had to ask to have."

Mrs. Chalk couldn't help herself. "Why don't you ask, then?" she inquired.

Mrs. Stobell started and eyed her indignantly. "So long as I had him I didn't want anything else," she said, stiffly. "We were all in all to each other; he couldn't bear me out of his sight. I remember once, when I had gone to see my poor mother, he sent me three telegrams in thirty-five minutes telling me to come home."

"Thomas was so unselfish," murmured Mrs. Chalk. "I once stayed with my mother for six weeks and he never said a word."

An odd expression, transient but unmistakable, flitted across the face of the listener.

"It nearly broke his heart, though, poor dear," said Mrs. Chalk, glaring at her. "He said he had never had such a time in his life."

"I don't expect he had," said Mrs. Stobell, screwing up her small features.

Mrs. Chalk drew herself up in her chair. "What do you mean by that?" she demanded.

"I meant what he meant," replied Mrs. Stobell, with a little air of surprise.

Mrs. Chalk bit her lip, and her friend, turning her head, gazed long and mournfully at a large photograph of Mr. Stobell painted in oils, which stared stiffly down on them from the wall.

"He never caused me a moment's uneasiness," she said, tenderly. "I could trust him anywhere."

Mrs. Chalk gazed thoughtfully at the portrait. It was not a good likeness, but it was more like Mr. Stobell than anybody else in Binchester, a fact which had been of some use in allaying certain unworthy suspicions of Mr. Stobell the first time he saw it.

"Yes," said Mrs. Chalk, significantly, "I should think you could."

Mrs. Stobell, about to reply, caught the staring eye of the photograph, and, shaking her head sorrowfully, took out her handkerchief and wiped her eyes. Mrs. Chalk softened.

"They both had their faults," she said, gently, "but they were great friends. I dare say that it was a comfort to them to be together to the last."

Captain Bowers himself began to lose hope at last, and went about in so moody a fashion that a shadow seemed to have fallen upon the cottage. By tacit consent the treasure had long been a forbidden subject, and even when the news of Selina's promissory note reached Dialstone Lane he had refused to discuss it. It had nothing to do with him, he said, and he washed his hands of it—a conclusion highly satisfactory to Miss Vickers, who had feared that she would have had to have dropped for a time her visits to Mr. Tasker.

A slight change in the household occurring at this time helped to divert the captain's thoughts. Mr. Tasker while chopping wood happened to chop his knee by mistake, and, as he did everything with great thoroughness, injured himself so badly that he had to be removed to his home. He was taken away at ten in the morning, and at a quarter-past eleven Selina Vickers, in a large apron and her sleeves rolled up over her elbows, was blacking the kitchen stove and throwing occasional replies to the objecting captain over her shoulder.

"I promised Joseph," she said, sharply, "and I don't break my promises for nobody. He was worrying about what you'd do all alone, and I told him I'd come."

Captain Bowers looked at her helplessly.

"I can manage very well by myself," he said, at last.

"Chop your leg off, I s'pose?" retorted Miss Vickers, good-temperedly. "Oh, you men!"

"And I'm not at home much while Miss Drewitt is away," added the captain.

"All the better," said Miss Vickers, breathing noisily on the stove and polishing with renewed vigour. "You won't be in my way."

The captain pulled himself together.

"You can finish what you're doing," he said, mildly, "and then—"

"Yes, I know what to do," interrupted Miss Vickers. "You leave it to me. Go in and sit down and make yourself comfortable. You ought not to be in the kitchen at all by rights. Not that I mind what people say—I should have enough to do if I did—but still—"

The captain fled in disorder and at first had serious thoughts of wiring for Miss Drewitt, who was spending a few days with friends in town. Thinking better of this, he walked down to a servants' registry office, and, after being shut up for a quarter of an hour in a small room with a middle-aged lady of Irish extraction, who was sent in to be catechized, resolved to let matters remain as they were.

Miss Vickers swept and dusted, cooked and scrubbed, undisturbed, and so peaceable was his demeanour when he returned from a walk one morning, and found the front room being "turned out," that she departed from her usual custom and explained the necessities of the case at some length.

"I dare say it'll be the better for it," said the captain.

"O' course it will," retorted Selina. "You don't think I'd do it for pleasure, do you? I thought you'd sit out in the garden, and of course it must come on to rain."

The captain said it didn't matter.

"Joseph," said Miss Vickers, as she squeezed a wet cloth into her pail— "Joseph's got a nice leg. It's healing very slow."

The captain, halting by the kitchen door, said he was sorry to hear it.

"Though there's worse things than bad legs," continued Miss Vickers, soaping her scrubbing-brush mechanically; "being lost at sea, for instance."

Captain Bowers made no reply. Adopting the idea that all roads lead to Rome, Miss Vickers had, during her stay at Dialstone Lane, made many indirect attempts to introduce the subject of the treasure-seekers.

"I suppose those gentlemen are drowned?" she said, bending down and scrubbing noisily.

The captain, taking advantage of her back being turned towards him, eyed her severely. The hardihood of the girl was appalling. His gaze wandered from her to the bureau, and, as his eye fell on the key sticking up in the lid, the idea of reading her a much-needed lesson presented itself. He stepped over the pail towards the bureau and, catching the girl's eye as she looked up, turned the key noisily in the lock and placed it ostentatiously in his pocket. A sudden vivid change in Selina's complexion satisfied him that his manoeuvre had been appreciated.

"Are you afraid I shall steal anything?" she demanded, hotly, as he regained the kitchen.

The captain quailed. "No," he said, hastily. "Somebody once took a paper of mine out of there, though," he added. "So I keep it locked up now."

Miss Vickers dropped the brush in the pail, and, rising slowly to her feet, stood wiping her hands on her coarse apron. Her face was red and white in patches, and the captain, regarding her with growing uneasiness, began to take in sail.

"At least, I thought they did," he muttered.

Selina paid no heed. "Get out o' my kitchen," she said, in a husky voice, as she brushed past him.

The captain obeyed hastily, and, stepping inside the dismantled room, stood for some time gazing out of window at the rain. Then he filled his pipe and, removing a small chair which was sitting upside down in a large one, took its place and stared disconsolately at the patch of wet floor and the general disorder.

At the end of an hour he took a furtive peep into the kitchen. Selina Vickers was sitting with her back towards him, brooding over the stove. It seemed clear to him that she was ashamed to meet his eye, and, glad to see such signs of grace in her, he resolved to spare her further confusion by going upstairs. He went up noisily and closed his door with a bang, but although he opened it afterwards and stood listening acutely he heard so sound from below.

By the end of the second hour his uneasiness had increased to consternation. The house was as silent as a tomb, the sitting-room was still in a state of chaos, and a healthy appetite would persist in putting ominous and inconvenient questions as to dinner. Whistling a cheerful air he went downstairs again and put his head in at the kitchen. Selina sat in the same attitude, and when he coughed made no response.

"What about dinner?" he said, at last, in a voice which strove to be unconcerned.

"Go away," said Selina, thickly. "I don't want no dinner."

The captain started. "But I do," he said, feelingly.

"You'd better get it yourself, then," replied Miss Vickers, without turning her head. "I might steal a potato or something."

"Don't talk nonsense," said the other, nervously.

"I'm not a thief," continued Miss Vickers. "I work as hard as anybody in Binchester, and nobody can ever say that I took the value of a farthing from them. If I'm poor I'm honest."

"Everybody knows that," said the captain, with fervour.

"You said you didn't want the paper," said Selina, turning at last and regarding him fiercely. "I heard you with my own ears, else I wouldn't have taken it. And if they had come back you'd have had your share. You didn't want the treasure yourself and you didn't want other people to have it. And it wasn't yours, because I heard you say so."

"Very well, say no more about it," said the captain. "If anybody asks you can say that I knew you had it. Now go and put that back in the bureau."

He tossed the key on to the table, and Miss Vickers, after a moment's hesitation, turned with a gratified smile and took it up. The next hour he spent in his bedroom, the rapid evolutions of Miss Vickers as she passed from the saucepans to the sitting room and from the sitting-room back to the saucepans requiring plenty of sea room.

A week later she was one of the happiest people in Binchester. Edward Tredgold had received a cable from Auckland: "All safe; coming home," and she shared with Mrs. Chalk and Mrs. Stobell in the hearty congratulations of a large circle of friends. Her satisfaction was only marred by the feverish condition of Mr. Tasker immediately on receipt of the news.

CHAPTER XXI

Fortunately for their peace of mind, Mr. Chalk and his friends, safe on board the s.s. Silver Star, bound for home, had no idea that the story of the treasure had become public property. Since their message it had become the principal topic of conversation in the town, and, Miss Vickers being no longer under the necessity of keeping her share in the affair secret, Mr. William Russell was relieved of a reputation for untruthfulness under which he had long laboured.

Various religious and philanthropic bodies began to bestir themselves. Owing to his restlessness and love of change no fewer than three sects claimed Mr. Chalk as their own, and, referring to his donations in the past, looked forward to a golden future. The claim of the Church to Mr. Tredgold was regarded as flawless, but the case of Mr. Stobell bristled with difficulties. Apologists said that he belonged to a sect unrepresented in Binchester, but an offshoot of the Baptists put in a claim on the ground that he had built that place of worship—at a considerable loss on the contract—some fifteen years before.

Dialstone Lane, when it became known that Captain Bowers had waived his claim to a share, was besieged by people seeking the reversion, and even Mint Street was not overlooked. Mr. Vickers repelled all callers with acrimonious impartiality, but Selina, after a long argument with a lady subaltern of the Salvation Army, during which the methods and bonnets of that organization were hotly assailed, so far relented as to present her with twopence on account.

Miss Drewitt looked forward to the return of the adventurers with disdainful interest. To Edward Tredgold she referred with pride to the captain's steadfast determination not to touch a penny of their ill-gotten gains, and with a few subtle strokes drew a comparison between her uncle and his father which he felt to be somewhat highly coloured. In extenuation he urged the rival claims of Chalk and Stobell.

"They were both led away by Chalk's eloquence and thirst for adventure," he said, as he walked by her side down the garden.

Miss Drewitt paid no heed. "And you will benefit by it," she remarked.

Mr. Tredgold drew himself up with an air the nobleness of which was somewhat marred by the expression of his eyes. "I will never touch a penny of it," he declared. "I will be like the captain. I am trying all I can to model myself on his lines."

The girl regarded him with suspicion. "I see no signs of any result at present," she said, coldly.

Mr. Tredgold smiled modestly. "Don't flatter me," he entreated.

"Flatter you!" said the indignant Prudence.

"On my consummate powers of concealment," was the reply. "I am keeping everything dark until I am so like him—in every particular—that you will not know the difference. I have often envied him the possession of such a niece. When the likeness is perfec——"

"Well?" said Miss Drewitt, with impatient scorn.

"You will have two uncles instead of one," rejoined Mr. Tredgold, impressively.

Miss Drewitt, with marked deliberation, came to a pause in the centre of the path.

"Are you going to continue talking nonsense?" she inquired, significantly.

Mr. Tredgold sighed. "I would rather talk sense," he replied, with a sudden change of manner.

"Try," said the girl, encouragingly.

"Only it is so difficult," said Edward, thoughtfully, "to you."

Miss Drewitt stopped again.

"For me," added the other, hastily. His companion said that she supposed it was. She also reminded him that nothing was easy without practice.

"And I ought not to find it difficult," complained Mr. Tredgold. "I have got plenty of sense hidden away somewhere."

Miss Drewitt permitted herself a faint exclamation of surprise. "It was not an empty boast of yours just now, then," she said.

"Boast?" repeated the other, blankly. "What boast?"

"On your wonderful powers of concealment," said Prudence, gently.

"You are reverting of your own accord to the nonsense," said Mr. Tredgold, sternly. "You are returning to the subject of uncles."

"Nothing of the kind," said Prudence, hotly.

"Before we leave it—forever," said Mr. Tredgold, dramatically, "I should like, if I am permitted, to make just one more remark on the subject. I would not, for all the wealth of this world, be your uncle Where are you going?"

"Indoors," said Miss Drewitt, briefly.

"One moment," implored the other. "I am just going to begin to talk sense."

"I will listen when you have had some practice," said the girl, walking towards the house.

"It's impossible to practise this," said Edward, following. "It is something that can only be confided to yourself. Won't you stay?"

"No," said the girl.

"Not from curiosity?"

Miss Drewitt, gazing steadfastly before her, shook her head.

"Well, perhaps I can say it as well indoors," murmured Edward, resignedly.

"And you'll have a bigger audience," said Prudence, breathing more easily as she reached the house. "Uncle is indoors."

She passed through the kitchen and into the sitting-room so hastily that Captain Bowers, who was sitting by the window reading, put down his paper and looked up in surprise. The look of grim determination on Mr. Tredgold's face did not escape him.

"Mr. Tredgold has come indoors to talk sense," said Prudence, demurely.

"Talk sense?" repeated the astonished captain.

"That's what he says," replied Miss Drewitt, taking a low chair by the captain's side and gazing composedly at the intruder. "I told him that you would like to hear it."

She turned her head for a second to hide her amusement, and in that second Mr. Tredgold favoured the captain with a glance the significance of which was at once returned fourfold. She looked up just in time to see their features relaxing, and moving nearer to the captain instinctively placed her hand upon his knee.

"I hope," said Captain Bowers, after a long and somewhat embarrassing silence—"I hope the conversation isn't going to be above my head?"

"Mr. Tredgold was talking about uncles," said Prudence, maliciously.

"Nothing bad about them, I hope?" said the captain, with pretended anxiety.

Edward shook his head. "I was merely envying Miss Drewitt her possession of you," he said, carelessly, "and I was just about to remark that I wished you were my uncle too, when she came indoors. I suppose she wanted you to hear it."

Miss Drewitt started violently, and her cheek flamed at the meanness of the attack.

"I wish I was, my lad," said the admiring captain.

"It would be the proudest moment of my life," said Edward, deliberately.

"And mine," said the captain, stoutly.

"And the happiest."

The captain bowed. "Same here," he said, graciously.

Miss Drewitt, listening helplessly to this fulsome exchange of compliments, wondered whether they had got to the end. The captain looked at Mr. Tredgold as though to remind him that it was his turn.

"You—you were going to show me a photograph of your first ship," said the latter, after a long pause. "Don't trouble if it's upstairs."

"It's no trouble," said the captain, briskly.

He rose to his feet and the hand of the indignant Prudence, dislodged from his knee, fell listlessly by her side. She sat upright, with her pale, composed face turned towards Mr. Tredgold. Her eyes were scornful and her lips slightly parted. Before these signs his courage flickered out and left him speechless. Even commonplace statements of fact were denied him. At last in sheer desperation he referred to the loudness of the clock's ticking.

"It seems to me to be the same as usual," said the girl, with a slight emphasis on the pronoun.

The clock ticked on undisturbed. Upstairs the amiable captain did his part nobly. Drawers opened and closed noisily; doors shut and lids of boxes slammed. The absurdity of the situation became unbearable, and despite her indignation at the treatment she had received Miss Drewitt felt a strong inclination to laugh. She turned her head swiftly and looked out of window, and the next moment Edward Tredgold crossed and took the captain's empty chair.

"Shall I call him down?" he asked, in a low voice.

"Call him down?" repeated the girl, coldly, but without turning her head. "Yes, if you——"

A loud crash overhead interrupted her sentence. It was evident that in his zeal the captain had pulled out a loaded drawer too far and gone over with it. Slapping sounds, as of a man dusting himself down, followed, and it was obvious that Miss Drewitt was only maintaining her gravity by a tremendous effort. Much emboldened by this fact the young man took her hand.

"Mr. Tredgold!" she said, in a stifled voice.

Undismayed by his accident the indefatigable captain was at it again, and in face of the bustle upstairs Prudence Drewitt was afraid to trust herself to say more. She sat silent with her head resolutely averted, but Edward took comfort in the fact that she had forgotten to withdraw her hand.

"Bless him!" he said, fervently, a little later, as the captain's foot was heard heavily on the stair. "Does he think we are deaf?"

CHAPTER XXII

Much to the surprise of their friends, who had not expected them home until November or December, telegrams were received from the adventurers, one day towards the end of September, announcing that they had landed at the Albert Docks and were on their way home by the earliest train. The most agreeable explanation of so short a voyage was that, having found the treasure, they had resolved to return home by steamer, leaving the Fair Emily to return at her leisure. But Captain Bowers, to whom Mrs. Chalk propounded this solution, suggested several others.

He walked down to the station in the evening to see the train come in, his curiosity as to the bearing and general state of mind of the travellers refusing to be denied. He had intended to witness the arrival from a remote corner of the platform, but to his surprise it was so thronged with sightseers that the precaution was unnecessary. The news of the return had spread like wildfire, and half Binchester had congregated to welcome their fellow-townsmen and congratulate them upon their romantically acquired wealth.

Despite the crowd the captain involuntarily shrank back as the train rattled into the station. The carriage containing the travellers stopped almost in front of him, and their consternation and annoyance at the extent of their reception were plainly visible. Bronzed and healthy-looking, they stepped out on to the platform, and after a brief greeting to Mrs. Chalk and Mrs. Stobell led the way in some haste to the exit. The crowd pressed close behind, and inquiries as to the treasure and its approximate value broke clamorously upon the ears of the maddened Mr. Stobell. Friends of many years who sought for particulars were shouldered aside, and it was left to Mr. Chalk, who struggled along in the rear with his wife, to announce that they had been shipwrecked.

Captain Bowers, who had just caught the word, heard the full particulars from him next day. For once the positions were reversed, and Mr. Chalk, who had so often sat in that room listening to the captain's yarns, swelled with pride as he noted the rapt fashion in which the captain listened to his. The tale of the shipwreck he regarded as a disagreeable necessity: a piece of paste flaunting itself among gems. In a few words he told how the Fair Emily crashed on to a reef in the middle of the night, and how, owing to the darkness and confusion, the boat into which he had got with Stobell and Tredgold was cast adrift; how a voice raised to a shriek cried to them to pull away, and how a minute afterwards the schooner disappeared with all hands.

"It almost unnerved me," he said, turning to Miss Drewitt, who was listening intently.

"You are sure she went down, I suppose?" said the captain; "she didn't just disappear in the darkness?"

"Sank like a stone," said Mr. Chalk, decidedly. "Our boat was nearly swamped in the vortex. Fortunately, the sea was calm, and when day broke we saw a small island about three miles away on our weather-beam."

"Where?" inquired Edward Tredgold, who had just looked in on the way to the office. Mr. Chalk explained.

"You tell the story much better than my father does," said Edward, nodding. "From the way he tells it one might think that you had the island in the boat with you."

Mr. Chalk started nervously. "It was three miles away on our weather-beam," he repeated, "the atmosphere clear and the sea calm. We sat down to a steady pull, and made the land in a little under the hour."

"Who did the pulling?" inquired Edward, casually.

Mr. Chalk started again, and wondered who had done it in Mr. Tredgold's version. He resolved to see him as soon as possible and arrange details.

"Most of us took a turn at it," he said, evasively, "and those who didn't encouraged the others."

"Most of you!" exclaimed the bewildered captain; "and those who didn't— but how many?"

"The events of that night are somewhat misty," interrupted Mr. Chalk, hastily. "The suddenness of the calamity and the shock of losing our shipmates—"

"It's wonderful to me that you can remember so much," said Edward, with a severe glance at the captain.

Mr. Chalk paid no heed. Having reached the island, the rest was truth and plain sailing. He described their life there until they were taken off by a trading schooner from Auckland, and how for three months they cruised with her among the islands. He spoke learnedly of atolls, copra, and missionaries, and, referring for a space to the Fijian belles, thought that their charms had been much overrated. Edward Tredgold, waiting until the three had secured berths in the s.s. *Silver Star*, trading between Auckland and London, took his departure.

Miss Vickers, who had been spending the day with a friend at Dutton Priors, and had missed the arrival in consequence, heard of the disaster in a mingled state of wrath and despair. The hopes of a year were shattered in a second, and, rejecting with fierceness the sympathy of her family, she went up to her room and sat brooding in the darkness.

She came down the next morning, pale from want of sleep. Mr. Vickers, who was at breakfast, eyed her curiously until, meeting her gaze in return, he blotted it out with a tea-cup.

"When you've done staring," said his daughter, "you can go upstairs and make yourself tidy."

"Tidy?" repeated Mr. Vickers. "What for?"

"I'm going to see those three," replied Selina, grimly; "and I want a witness. And I may as well have a clean one while I'm about it."

Mr. Vickers darted upstairs with alacrity, and having made himself approximately tidy smoked a morning pipe on the doorstep while his daughter got ready. An air of importance and dignity suitable to the occasion partly kept off inquirers.

"We'll go and see Mr. Stobell first," said his daughter, as she came out.

"Very good," said the witness, "but if you asked my advice——"

"You just keep quiet," said Selina, irritably; "I've not gone quite off my head yet. And don't hum!"

Mr. Vickers lapsed into offended silence, and, arrived at Mr. Stobell's, followed his daughter into the hall in so stately a fashion that the maid—lately of Mint Street—implored him not to eat her. Miss Vickers replied for him, and the altercation that ensued was only quelled by the appearance of Mr. Stobell at the dining-room door.

"Halloa! What do you want?" he inquired, staring at the intruders.

"I've come for my share," said Miss Vickers, eyeing him fiercely.

"Share?" repeated Mr. Stobell. "Share? Why, we've been shipwrecked. Haven't you heard?"

"Perhaps you came to my house when I wasn't at home," retorted Miss Vickers, in a trembling but sarcastic voice. "I want to hear about it. That's what I've come for."

She walked to the dining-room and, as Mr. Stobell still stood in the doorway, pushed past him, followed by her father. Mr. Stobell, after a short deliberation, returned to his seat at the breakfast-table, and in an angry and disjointed fashion narrated the fate of the Fair Emily and their subsequent adventures. Miss Vickers heard him to an end in silence.

"What time was it when the ship struck on the rock?" she inquired.

Mr. Stobell stared at her. "Eleven o'clock," he said, gruffly.

Miss Vickers made a note in a little red-covered memorandum-book.

"Who got in the boat first?" she demanded.

Mr. Stobell's lips twisted in a faint grin. "Chalk did," he said, with relish.

Miss Vickers, nodding at the witness to call his attention to the fact, made another note.

"How far was the boat off when the ship sank?"

"Here, look here—" began the indignant Stobell.

"How far was the boat off?" interposed the witness, severely; "that's what we want to know."

"You hold your tongue," said his daughter.

"I'm doing the talking. How far was the boat off?"

"About four yards," replied Mr. Stobell. "And now look here; if you want to know any more, you go and see Mr. Chalk. I'm sick and tired of the whole business. And you'd no right to talk about it while we were away."

"I've got the paper you signed and I'm going to know the truth," said Miss Vickers, fiercely. "It's my right. What was the size of the island?"

Mr. Stobell maintained an obstinate silence.

"What colour did you say these 'ere Fidgetty islanders was?" inquired Mr. Vickers, with truculent curiosity.

"You get out," roared Stobell, rising. "At once. D'ye hear me?"

Mr. Vickers backed with some haste towards the door. His daughter followed slowly.

"I don't believe you," she said, turning sharply on Stobell. "I don't believe the ship was wrecked at all."

Mr. Stobell sat gasping at her. "What?" he stammered. "W h-a-a-t?"

"I don't believe it was wrecked," repeated Selina, wildly. "You've got the treasure all right, and you're keeping it quiet and telling this tale to do me out of my share. I haven't done with you yet. You wait!"

She flung out into the hall, and Mr. Vickers, after a lofty glance at Mr. Stobell, followed her outside.

"And now we'll go and hear what Mr. Tredgold has to say," she said, as they walked up the road. "And after that, Mr. Chalk."

Mr. Tredgold was just starting for the office when they arrived, but, recognising the justice of Miss Vickers's request for news, he stopped and gave his version of the loss of the Fair Emily. In several details it differed from that of Mr. Stobell, and he looked at her uneasily as she took out pencil and paper and made notes.

"If you want any further particulars you had better go and see Mr. Stobell," he said, restlessly. "I am busy."

"We've just been to see him," replied Miss Vickers, with an ominous gleam in her eye. "You say that the boat was two or three hundred yards away when the ship sank?"

"More or less," was the cautious reply.

"Mr. Stobell said about half a mile," suggested the wily Selina.

"Well, perhaps that would be more correct," said the other.

"Half a mile, then?"

"Half a mile," said Mr. Tredgold, nodding, as she wrote it down.

"Four yards was what Mr. Stobell said," exclaimed Selina, excitedly. "I've got it down here, and father heard it. And you make the time it happened and a lot of other things different. I don't believe that you were any more shipwrecked than I was."

"Not so much," added the irrepressible Mr. Vickers.

Mr. Tredgold walked to the door. "I am busy," he said, curtly. "Good morning."

Miss Vickers passed him with head erect, and her small figure trembling with rage and determination. By the time she had cross-examined Mr. Chalk her wildest suspicions were confirmed. His account differed in several particulars from the others, and his alarm and confusion when taxed with the discrepancies were unmistakable.

Binchester rang with the story of her wrongs, and, being furnished with three different accounts of the same incident, seemed inclined to display a little pardonable curiosity. To satisfy this, intimates of the gentlemen most concerned were provided with an official version, which Miss Vickers discovered after a little research was compiled for the most part by adding all the statements together and dividing by three. She paid another round of visits to tax them with the fact, and, strong in the justice of her cause, even followed them in the street demanding her money.

"There's one comfort," she said to the depressed Mr. Tasker. "I've got you, Joseph. They can't take you away from me."

"There's nobody could do that," responded Mr. Tasker, with a sigh of resignation.

"And if I had to choose," continued Miss Vickers, putting her arm round his waist, "I'd sooner have you than a hundred thousand pounds."

Mr. Tasker sighed again at the idea of an article estimated at so high a figure passing into the possession of Selina Vickers. In a voice broken with emotion he urged her to persevere in her claims to a fortune which he felt would alone make his fate tolerable. The unsuspecting Selina promised.

"She'll quiet down in time," said Captain Bowers to Mr. Chalk, after the latter had been followed nearly all the way to Dialstone Lane by Miss Vickers, airing her grievance and calling upon him to remedy it. "Once she realizes the fact that the ship is lost, she'll be all right."

Mr. Chalk looked unconvinced. "She doesn't want to realize it," he said, shaking his head.

"She'll be all right in time," repeated the captain; "and after all, you know," he added, with gentle severity, "you deserve to suffer a little. You had no business with that map."

CHAPTER XXIII

On a fine afternoon towards the end of the following month Captain Brisket and Mr. Duckett sat outside the Swan and Bottle Inn, Holemouth, a small port forty miles distant from Biddlecombe. The day was fine, with just a touch of crispness in the air to indicate the waning of the year, and, despite a position regarded by the gloomy Mr. Duckett as teeming with perils, the captain turned a bright and confident eye on the *Fair Emily*, anchored in the harbour.

"We ought to have gone straight to Biddlecombe," said Mr. Duckett, following his glance; "it would have looked better. Not that anything'll make much difference."

"And everybody in a flutter of excitement telegraphing off to the owners," commented the captain. "No, we'll tell our story first; quiet and comfortable-like. Say it over again."

"I've said it three times," objected Mr. Duckett; "and each time it sounds more unreal than ever."

"It'll be all right," said Brisket, puffing at his cigar. "Besides, we've got no choice. It's that or ruin, and there's nobody within thousands of miles to contradict us. We bring both the ship and the map back to 'em. What more can they ask?"

"You'll soon know," said the pessimistic Mr. Duckett. "I wonder whether they'll have another shot for the treasure when they get that map back?" "I should like to send that Captain Bowers out searching for it," said Brisket, scowling, "and keep him out there till he finds it. It's all his fault. If it hadn't been for his cock-and-bull story we shouldn't ha' done what we did. Hanging's too good for him."

"I suppose it's best for them not to know that there's no such island?" hazarded Mr. Duckett.

"O' course," snapped his companion. "Looks better for us, don't it, giving them back a map worth half a million. Now go through the yarn again and I'll see whether I can pick any holes in it. The train goes in half an hour."

Mr. Duckett sighed and, first emptying his mug, began a monotonous recital. Brisket listened attentively.

"We were down below asleep when the men came running down and overpowered us. They weighed anchor at night, and following morning made you, by threats, promise to steer them to the island. You told me on the quiet that you'd die before you betrayed the owners' trust. How did they know that the island the gentlemen were on wasn't the right one? Because Sam Betts was standing by when you told me you'd made a mistake in your reckoning and said we'd better go ashore and tell them."

"That's all right so far, I think," said Brisket, nodding.

"We sailed about and tried island after island just to satisfy the men and seize our opportunity," continued Mr. Duckett, with a weary air. "At last, one day, when they were all drunk ashore, we took the map, shipped these natives, and sailed back to the island to rescue the owners. Found they'd gone when we got there. Mr. Stobell's boot and an old pair of braces produced in proof."

"Better wrap it up in a piece o' newspaper," said Brisket, stooping and producing the relic in question from under the table.

"Shipped four white men at Viti Levu and sailed for home," continued Mr. Duckett. "Could have had more, but wanted to save owners' pockets, and worked like A.B.'s ourselves to do so."

"Let'em upset that if they can," said Brisket, with a confident smile. "The crew are scattered, and if they happened to get one of them it's only his word against ours. Wait a bit. How did the crew know of the treasure?"

"Chalk told you," responded the obedient Duckett. "And if he told you —and he can't deny it—why not them?"

Captain Briskett nodded approval. "It's all right as far as I can see," he said, cautiously. "But mind. Leave the telling of it to me. You can just chip in with little bits here and there. Now let's get under way."

He threw away the stump of his cigar and rose, turning as he reached the corner for a lingering glance at the Fair Emily.

"Scrape her and clean her and she'd be as good as ever," he said, with a sigh. "She's just the sort o' little craft you and me could ha' done with, Peter."

They had to change twice on the way to Binchester, and at each stopping-place Mr. Duckett, a prey to nervousness, suggested the wisdom of disappearing while they had the opportunity.

"Disappear and starve, I suppose?" grunted the scornful Brisket. "What about my certificate? and yours, too? I tell you it's our only chance."

He walked up the path to Mr. Chalk's house with a swagger which the mate endeavoured in vain to imitate. Mr. Chalk was out, but the captain, learning that he was probably to be found at Dialstone Lane, decided to follow him there rather than first take his tidings to Stobell or Tredgold. With the idea of putting Mr. Duckett at his ease he talked on various matters as they walked, and, arrived at Dialstone Lane, even stopped to point out the picturesque appearance its old houses made in the moonlight.

"This is where the old pirate who made the map lives," he whispered, as he reached the door. "If he's got anything to say I'll tackle him about that. Now, pull yourself together!"

He knocked loudly on the door with his fist. A murmur of voices stopped suddenly, and, in response to a gruff command from within, he opened the door and stood staring at all three of his victims, who were seated at the table playing whist with Captain Bowers.

The three gentlemen stared back in return. Tredgold and Chalk had half risen from their seats; Mr. Stobell, with both arms on the table, leaned forward, and regarded him open-mouthed.

"Good evening, gentlemen all," said Captain Brisket, in a hearty voice.

He stepped forward, and seizing Mr. Chalk's hand wrung it fervently.

"It's good for sore eyes to see you again, sir," he said. "Look at him, Peter!"

Mr. Duckett, ignoring this reflection on his personal appearance, stepped quietly inside the door, and stood smiling nervously at the company.

"It's him," said the staring Mr. Stobell, drawing a deep breath. "It's Brisket."

He pushed his chair back and, rising slowly from the table, confronted him. Captain Brisket, red-faced and confident, stared up at him composedly.

"It's Brisket," said Mr. Stobell again, in a voice of deep content. "Turn the key in that door, Chalk."

Mr. Chalk hesitated, but Brisket, stepping to the door, turned the key and, placing it on the table, returned to his place by the side of the mate. Except for a hard glint in his eye his face still retained its smiling composure.

"And now," said Stobell, "you and me have got a word or two to say to each other. I haven't had the pleasure of seeing your ugly face since—"

"Since the disaster," interrupted Tredgold, loudly and hastily.

"Since the—"

Mr. Stobell suddenly remembered. For a few moments he stood irresolute, and then, with an extraordinary contortion of visage, dropped into his chair again and sat gazing blankly before him.

"Me and Peter Duckett only landed to-day," said Brisket, "and we came on to see you by the first train we could—"

"I know," said Tredgold, starting up and taking his hand, "and we're delighted to see you are safe. And Mr. Duckett?—"

He found Mr. Duckett's hand after a little trouble—the owner seeming to think that he wanted it for some unlawful purpose—and shook that. Captain Brisket, considerably taken aback by this performance, gazed at him with suspicion.

"You didn't go down with your ship, then, after all," said Captain Bowers, who had been looking on with much interest.

Amazement held Brisket dumb. He turned and eyed Duckett inquiringly. Then Tredgold, with his back to the others, caught his eye and frowned significantly.

"If Captain Brisket didn't go down with it I am sure that he was the last man to leave it," he said, kindly;

"and Mr. Duckett last but one."

Mr. Duckett, distrustful of these compliments, cast an agonized glance at the door.

"Stobell was a bit rough just now," said Tredgold, with another warning glance at Brisket, "but he didn't like being shipwrecked."

Brisket gazed at the door in his turn. He had an uncomfortable feeling that he was being played with.

"It's nothing much to like," he said, at last, but—"

"Tell us how you escaped," said Tredgold; "or, perhaps," he continued, hastily, as Brisket was about to speak—"perhaps you would like first to hear how we did."

"Perhaps that would be better," said the perplexed Brisket.

He nudged the mate with his elbow, and Mr. Tredgold, still keeping him under the spell of his eye, began with great rapidity to narrate the circumstances attending the loss of the Fair Emily. After one irrepressible grunt of surprise Captain Brisket listened without moving a muscle, but the changes on Mr. Duckett's face were so extraordinary that on several occasions the narrator faltered and lost the thread of his discourse. At such times Mr. Chalk took up the story, and once, when both seemed at a loss, a growling contribution came from Mr. Stobell.

"Of course, you got away in the other boat," said Tredgold, nervously, when he had finished.

Brisket looked round shrewdly, his wits hard at work. Already the advantages of adopting a story which he supposed to have been concocted for the benefit of Captain Bowers were beginning to multiply in his ready brain.

"And didn't see us owing to the darkness," prompted Tredgold, with a glance at Mr. Joseph Tasker, who was lingering by the door after bringing in some whisky.

"You're quite right, sir," said Brisket, after a trying pause. "I didn't see you."

Unasked he took a chair, and with crossed legs and folded arms surveyed the company with a broad smile.

"You're a fine sort of shipmaster," exclaimed the indignant Captain Bowers. "First you throw away your ship, and then you let your passengers shift for themselves."

"I am responsible to my owners," said Brisket. "Have you any fault to find with me, gentlemen?" he demanded, turning on them with a frown.

Tredgold and Chalk hastened to reassure him.

"In the confusion the boat got adrift," said Brisket. "You've got their own word for it. Not that they didn't behave well for landsmen: Mr. Chalk's pluck was wonderful, and Mr. Tredgold was all right."

Mr. Stobell turned a dull but ferocious eye upon him.

"And you all got off in the other boat," said Tredgold. "I'm very glad."

Captain Brisket looked at him, but made no reply. The problem of how to make the best of the situation was occupying all his attention.

"Me and Peter Duckett would be glad of some of our pay," he said, at last.

"Pay?" repeated Tredgold, in a dazed voice.

Brisket looked at him again, and then gave a significant glance in the direction of Captain Bowers. "We'd like twenty pounds on account—now," he said, calmly.

Tredgold looked hastily at his friends. "Come and see me to-morrow," he said, nervously, "and we'll settle things."

"You can send us the rest," said Brisket, "but we want that now. We're off to-night."

"But we must see you again," said Tredgold, who was anxious to make arrangements about the schooner. "We—we've got a lot of things to talk about. The—the ship, for instance."

"I'll talk about her now if you want me to," said Brisket, with unpleasant readiness. "Meantime, we'd like that money."

Fortunately—or unfortunately—Tredgold had been to his bank that morning, and, turning a deaf ear to the expostulations of Captain Bowers, he produced his pocketbook, and after a consultation with Mr. Chalk, and an attempt at one with the raging Stobell, counted out the money and handed it over.

"And there is an I.O.U. for the remainder," he said, with an attempt at a smile, as he wrote on a slip of paper.

Brisket took it with pleased surprise, and the mate, leaning against his shoulder, read the contents: "*Where is the 'Fair Emily'?*"

"You might as well give me a receipt," said Tredgold, significantly, as he passed over pencil and paper.

Captain Brisket thanked him and, sucking the pencil, eyed him thoughtfully. Then he bent to the table and wrote.

"You sign here, Peter," he said.

Mr. Tredgold smiled at the precaution, but the smile faded when he took the paper. It was a correctly worded receipt for twenty pounds. He began to think that he had rated the captain's intelligence somewhat too highly.

"Ah, we've had a hard time of it," said Brisket, putting the notes into his breast-pocket and staring hard at Captain Bowers. "When that little craft went down, of course I went down with her. How I got up I don't know, but when I did there was Peter hanging over the side of the boat and pulling me in by the hair."

He paused to pat the mate on the shoulder.

"Unfortunately for us we took a different direction to you, sir," he continued, turning to Tredgold, "and we were pulling for six days before we were picked up by a barque bound for Melbourne. By the time she sighted us we were reduced to half a biscuit a day each and two teaspoonfuls o' water, and not a man grumbled. Did they, Peter?"

"Not a man," said Mr. Duckett.

"At Melbourne," said the captain, who was in a hurry to be off, "we all separated, and Duckett and me worked our way home on a cargo-boat. We always stick together, Peter and me."

"And always will," said Mr. Duckett, with a little emotion as he gazed meaningly at the captain's breast-pocket.

"When I think o' that little craft lying all those fathoms down," continued the captain, staring full at Mr. Tredgold, "it hurts me. The nicest little craft of her kind I ever handled. Well—so long, gentlemen."

"We shall see you to-morrow," said Tredgold, hastily, as the captain rose.

Brisket shook his head.

"Me and Peter are very busy," he said, softly. "We've been putting our little bit o' savings together to buy a schooner, and we want to settle things as soon as possible."

"A schooner?" exclaimed Mr. Tredgold, with an odd look.

Captain Brisket nodded indulgently.

"One o' the prettiest little craft you ever saw, gentlemen," he said," and, if you've got no objection, me and Peter Duckett thought o' calling her the *Fair Emily*, in memory of old times. Peter's a bit sentimental at times, but I don't know as I can blame him for it. Good night."

He opened the door slowly, and the sentimental Mr. Duckett, still holding fast to the parcel containing Mr. Stobell's old boot, slipped thankfully outside. Calmly and deliberately Captain Brisket followed, and the door was closing behind him when it suddenly stopped, and his red face was thrust into the room again.

"One thing is," he said, eyeing the speechless Tredgold with sly relish, "she's uncommonly like the Fair Emily we lost. Good night."

The door closed with a snap, but Tredgold and Chalk made no move. Glued to their seats, they stared blankly at the door, until the rigidity of their pose and the strangeness of their gaze began to affect the slower-witted Mr. Stobell.

"Anything wrong?" inquired the astonished Captain Bowers, looking from one to the other.

There was no reply. Mr. Stobell rose and, after steadying himself for a moment with his hands on the table, blundered heavily towards the door. As though magnetized, Tredgold and Chalk followed and, standing beside him on the footpath, stared solemnly up Dialstone Lane.

Captain Brisket and his faithful mate had disappeared.

W.W. Jacobs – A Short Biography

William Wymark Jacobs was born on September 8, 1863 in the Wapping district of London, England. An author, humorist and dramatist, Jacobs is best remembered for the enduring classic tale of horror - "The Monkey's Paw".

As a youth, Jacobs grew up near the Wapping docks in London, where his father was a wharf manager. The family's first home was home was a house on a River Thames wharf.

The docklands setting would show up frequently in his later literary output. Jacobs, the wharf rat, and his three siblings lost their mother when they were all still young children. Their father, William Gage Jacobs, remarried and fathered a further seven children with his erstwhile housekeeper Ellen Florey. Although he grew up surrounded by poverty, Jacobs himself received a formal education in London, first at a private prep school and later at the Birkbeck Literary and Scientific Institute (now part of the University of London and known as Birkbeck College).

Jacobs' adult working life began with a clerical position at the Post Office Savings Bank. The job was not a stimulating one but Jacobs put his imagination to good use and started to write short stories, sketches and articles, many of which appeared in the Post Office house publication "Blackfriars Magazine."

Although Jacobs did receive his fair share of rejection slips at the beginning of his career, many works written during this period of clerical employment appeared in the "Idler" and "Today" magazines, both of which were edited by noted humorist Jerome K. Jerome, who had taken a liking to Jacobs' stories.

From 1898, Jacobs also published stories in "The Strand", a popular, monthly fiction and general interest magazine. The arrangement stayed in place for most of his life and many of the works in Jacobs' subsequent collections – including the nautical serialization A Master of Craft (1899-1900) - appeared there first.

Jacobs' first volume of collected works was published in 1896. Many Cargoes, a selection of sea-faring yarns, established Jacobs as a popular writer and humorist with a penchant for authentic dialogue and trick endings (critics of the day referred to him as the "O. Henry of the Waterfront").

A year later he published a novelette, The Skipper's Wooing, and in 1898 and another collection of short stories titled Sea Urchins. These works painted vivid, if imaginatively stretched, pictures of dockland and seafaring London with colourful characters (such as "The Night Watchman", Ginger Dick) that now seem archetypal.

Many of Jacobs' periodical publications and first editions were illustrated with woodcuts and ink drawings, as was still the custom at the turn of the 20th century. The author worked regularly with artists such as E.W. Kemble, who had illustrated Mark Twain's Adventures of Huckleberry Finn and Harriet Beecher Stowe's Uncle Tom's Cabin, and his good friend Will Owen, who eventually became a household name on the strength of his iconic Bisto Kids, Bovril and Lux Soap advertising posters.

By 1899, Jacobs was able to quit the post office and finally begin a career making a living as a full-time writer.

He married the noted suffragist Agnes Eleanor Williams (who had been jailed for her protest activities) in 1900. They set up a household in Loughton, Essex as well as living part of the year in central London. The couple went on to have five children together though their marriage was considered an unhappy one.

The publication of two short novels: At Sunwich Port (a romantic tale of rival sea captains in the fictional seaside community of Sunwich standing in for the actual East England community of Sandwich, Kent) and Dialstone Lane (another small town romance involving intrigue and buried treasure), in 1902 and 1904 respectively, cemented Jacobs' reputation as one of the leading British authors of the new century.

On the foundations of a continuing ability to write for his audience he was readily published though he never strayed too far from what was becoming his familiar, dependable style. There followed a string of further successful publications, including Captain's All (1905), Night Watches (1914), The Castaways (1916), and Sea Whispers (1926). Jacobs published eighteen books in all during his lifetime; thirteen collections and five novels.

As a storyteller, Jacobs is perhaps better remembered for a handful of brief tales of the supernatural than for his popular nautical-themed works. The most famous of these, The Monkey's Paw, originally appeared as part of the 1902 short story collection The Lady of the Barge. It is an economically written story about a shriveled talisman, a monkey's paw that brings grief and horror in the wake of all too literal wish granting. The story has been adapted for other media repeatedly, starting with a one-act play performed at London's Haymarket Theatre in 1903. There have been multiple film adaptations of the story in the modern era; some of us are familiar with its appearance in an episode of the popular animated series, The Simpsons.

Another macabre gem, The Toll-House, was published as part of the collection Sailor's Knots in 1909. Jacob's once again employs a sparse style to tell the story of a group of men who spend the night in a famously haunted house on a dare (a noticeably similar narrative concept was put to use in the much earlier play The Ghost of Jerry Bundler, which had launched Jacobs' parallel career as a dramatist back in 1899 when it was produced at the St. James Theatre in London). Innovative at the time of writing, these sparingly written, atmospheric ghost stories are now familiar classics of the supernatural genre.

Though prolific in his younger years, Jacobs' productivity dropped dramatically after the start of World War I. Yet even in self-imposed semi-retirement Jacobs was still recognized as a leading humorist, ranked alongside such writers as P. G. Wodehouse and George Birmingham. He enjoyed continuing influence and elevated status among his fellow writers as evidenced by these comments attributed to his colleague Henry James:

"Mr. Jacobs, I envy you. You are popular! Your admirable work is appreciated by a wide circle of readers;

it has achieved popularity. Mine never goes into a second edition."

James' literary fortunes would, of course, change, but his back-handedly complimentary admiration is compelling evidence of Jacobs' reputation as a writer and humourist both for his audience and his perhaps more admired literary colleagues.

Though Jacobs would create little in the way of new work after 1911, he was still writing. In these later years, seemingly burnt out creatively, Jacobs concentrated more on writing dramatizations and adaptations of his existing stories, including Beauty and the Barge (a film version starring Margaret Rutherford was also released in 1937) and In the Dark (a one act play that is often performed pr published with The Monkey's Paw adaptation).

Though admired by loyal readers throughout his lifetime, Jacobs has been almost completely forgotten since. Critics are at a loss to name a single reason why - Jacobs is universally considered to be a fine and imaginative literary craftsman. But, as critic John Wain suggested in a 1960 essay, perhaps Jacobs' humour may have been too gentle to persist into the cruel and sarcastic modern era, his dry pokes at proletariat hardship no longer suiting the times.

Nonetheless, Jacobs' legacy remains solid: he continued Dickens' (a writer with whom he is also often compared) tradition for sharing working class stories in authentic vernacular. And polished narratives such as The Monkey's Paw set a standard for the clever use of horror in fiction and popular culture that endures to this day. Indeed recently his works have begun to show an increased demand and appreciation in a world that is constantly looking over its shoulder.

William Wymark Jacobs died in a North London nursing home in Hornsey Lane, Islington on September 1st, 1943, just a week before his 80th birthday.

W.W. Jacobs – A Concise Bibliography

NOVELS AND SHORT STORY COLLECTIONS
MANY CARGOES (SHORT STORIES) (1896)
THE SKIPPER'S WOOING (1897)
SEA URCHINS (SHORT STORIES) (1898) aka MORE CARGOES
A MASTER OF CRAFT (1900)
LIGHT FREIGHTS (SHORT STORIES) (1901)
THE LADY OF THE BARGE (SHORT STORIES) (1902)
AT SUNWICH PORT (1902)
DIALSTONE LANE (1902)
SALTHAVEN (1908)
CAPTAINS ALL (SHORT STORIES) (1911)
NIGHT WATCHERS (SHORT STORIES) (1914)
DEEP WATERS (SHORT STORIES) (1919)

SHORT STORIES (INCLUDING THOSE USED IN THE COLLECTIONS ABOVE)
A BENEFIT PERFORMANCE

A BLACK AFFAIR
A CASE OF DESERTION
A CHANGE OF TREATMENT
A CIRCULAR TOUR
A DISCIPLINARIAN
A DISTANT RELATIVE
A GARDEN PLOT
A GOLDEN VENTURE
A HARBOUR OF REFUGE
A LOVE KNOT
A LOVE PASSAGE
A MARKED MAN
A MIXED PROPOSAL
A RASH EXPERIMENT
A SAFETY MATCH
A SPIRIT OF AVARICE
A TIGER'S SKIN
ADMIRAL PETERS
AFTER THE INQUEST
ALF'S DREAM
AN ADULTERATION ACT
AN ELABORATE ELOPEMENT
AN INTERVENTION
AN ODD FREAK
ANGELS' VISITS
BACK TO BACK
BEDRIDDEN
THE WINTER OFFENSIVE
THE BEQUEST
BILL'S LAPSE
BILL'S PAPER CHASE
BLUNDELL'S IMPROVEMENT
THE BOATSWAIN'S WATCH
THE BOATSWAIN'S MATE
BOB'S REDEMPTION
BREAKING A SPELL
BREVET RANK
BROTHER HUTCHINS
THE BULLY OF THE "CAVENDISH"
THE CABIN PASSENGER
CAPTAIN ROGERS
THE CAPTAIN'S EXPLOIT
CAPTAINS ALL
THE CASTAWAY
THE CHANGELING
"CHOICE SPIRITS"
THE CONSTABLE'S MOVE
CONTRABAND OF WAR

THE MONKEY'S PAW
MRS. BUNKER'S CHAPERON
THE NEST EGG
ODD MAN OUT
THE OLD MAN OF THE SEA
OUTSAILED
OVER THE SIDE
PAYING OFF
THE PERSECUTION OF BOB PRETTY
PETER'S PENCE
PICKLED HERRING
PRIVATE CLOTHES
PRIZE MONEY
THE RESURRECTION OF MR. WIGGETT
THE RIVAL BEAUTIES
RULE OF THREE
SAM'S BOY
SAM'S GHOST
SELF-HELP
SENTENCE DEFERRED
SHAREHOLDERS
SKILLED ASSISTANCE
THE SKIPPER OF THE "OSPREY"
SMOKED SKIPPER
STEPPING BACKWARDS
STRIKING HARD
THE SUBSTITUTE
THE TEMPTATION OF SAMUEL BURGE
THE TEST
THE THREE SISTERS
TO HAVE AND TO HOLD
"THE TOLL-HOUSE"
TWIN SPIRITS
TWO OF A TRADE
THE UNDERSTUDY
THE UNKNOWN
THE VIGIL
WATCH-DOGS
THE WEAKER VESSEL
THE WELL
THE WHITE CAT

STAGE
THE GHOST OF JERRY BUNDLER (1899) (In London)

FILM ADAPTATIONS

A MASTER OF CRAFT (1922)
THE MONKEY'S PAW (1933)
OUR RELATIONS, a Laurel & Hardy film, "suggested by" to Jacobs' "The Money Box." (1936)
FOOTSTEPS IN THE FOG, from the short story The Interruption. (1955)

www.ingramcontent.com/pod-product-compliance
Lightning Source LLC
Chambersburg PA
CBHW071352170626
46811CB00003B/1103